Sanitarium Magazine
Issue no. 7

First Published 2013 by Sanitarium Press

This edition published 2021 by Sanitarium Publishing

ISBN 9798706394110

Facebook: https://www.facebook.com/SanitariumPublishing

Website: https://www.thesanitarium.co.uk/

2013 Edition edited by Barry Skelhorn

2021 Edition by Ian Sputnik

Thank you to all of our contributors, we couldn't have done it without you.

Contents

ISSUE SEVEN

Welcome to Sanitarium #007.
We have an insightful moment with Mark Tufo, we see where the horror happens with Richard Thomas and we have nine stories to share with you.

So here is to the future of Sanitarium.

Barry Skelhorn

Case File: #50395

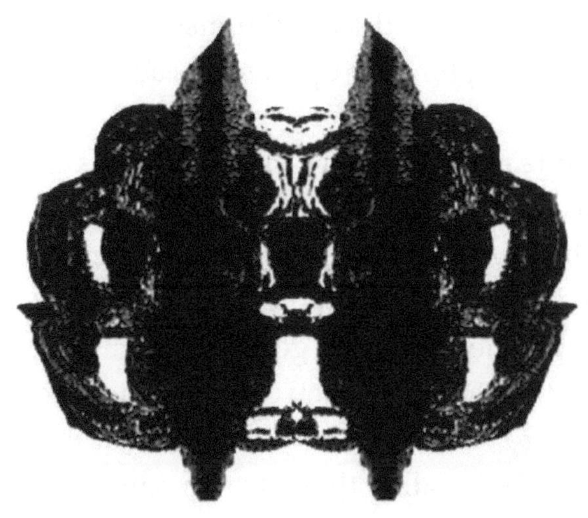

Beneath the Flesh by Philip Roberts

Roy's days of fixing leaks, showing rooms, running down people behind on rent, and filing paperwork always ended on his balcony with a six pack by his feet.

Only two of the five parking lot lights actually turned on in the gloomy twilight. Cicadas filled the night with their chirping while the muggy air brought sweat to both Roy's face and the cold can of beer in his grip.

Halfway through the can he heard the crunch of feet on gravel and saw a person walking through the darkness. He sat back and watched with indifference until he saw them turn towards apartment 605. Only then did he lean forward a little more, arms on the railing to his balcony, watching them open the door and slip inside.

Slumped back in his seat again he frowned at the apartment. "Who rents that?" he quietly asked himself. A sigh preceded the grunt of him pulling himself up to step back into his office and home.

He took a bite from an open candy bar on his desk as he knelt before his files and started flipping through them. Most of the rooms had already been rented out before he'd purchased the place, but he'd eventually seen the various renters, either when they left, or when he needed to go fix something.

File in hand, he stepped back out onto his balcony and took up a seat, only to find the folder was almost empty. More he thought about it he recalled they always paid cash, too.

Roy liked to be aware of the trouble he might be dealing with eventually, and right then, leaning forward again on the guardrails, he frowned at 605. Images began coming to him of other people passing through that door, quite a few from time to time.

On a whim he hefted his bulk out of the chair and made his way through his apartment, out the door, down the stairs, and across the way to the door of 605.

There weren't any working lights near the door, leaving Roy in almost total darkness. He knocked twice.

"This is the owner," he shouted. "Got a call about a noise complaint. Wanted to check it out."

Without a light from in the apartment he could barely make out the man who peered out at him, visible only in the crack of the open door. "What noise?" he asked, voice a little slurred, kind of wet, Roy thought.

"Just got a call. Wanted to make sure everything was ok."

The door opened completely, revealed the man and the odd nature to his face. "There was no call," he said, but his face didn't seem to move very well with the words, almost as if he'd injected some kind of anesthesia into his skin.

Roy offered the man a yellow-toothed smile. "No, there wasn't a call. Like to know my tenants. What's with your face?"

It took a few seconds for the smell to reach him, coming from the apartment; so vile he had to wrinkle his nose.

The man's head cocked to the side, his eyes glistening, too sunken back in his face, Roy thought. "How old are you, Mr. Burler," he asked.

Roy couldn't say what bothered him the most: the smell, the creepy look of the man's face, or maybe that he'd known Roy's last name. "Look, sorry I bothered you." He turned from the stranger, felt the eyes still watching him until he'd made it to the stairs leading up to his room. Only then did he turn back to see the door closing, but he could still see in his mind the voice speaking without the lips moving, words slurred, warped.

"I don't need this," he whispered as he trudged up the stairs.

***

He started keeping an eye on the place, and told Hector Bedney, a guy he hired to help maintain the complex, to do the same. Three people entered the apartment that week, and in the evenings, after seeing a girl duck through the door, Roy waited up six hours, and yet never saw her leave.

"You ever actually see those people walk out?" he asked Hector on a smoke break.

The younger man scrunched up his face in careful consideration before shaking his head. "You know, don't think I have. What you think they're doing in there?"

"Wish I knew. That's what's eating at me. I haven't any clue. Guy I talked to had to be on drugs of some kind, but couldn't say what kind, and where are all the people going?"

Hector only shrugged; his purposeful disinterest clear. He'd always done his best to stay out of the affairs of the people Roy rented out rooms to. Once Roy knew the affairs themselves, he didn't mind staying away as well, but the idea of not knowing bugged him.

The note showed up on the inside of his front door a little over two weeks after he'd first gone to 605. Wearing only a pair of stained boxers and a thin robe, he walked cautiously up to the note, checking to see the deadbolt was still in place before pulling the paper from his door.

"You're forty-four years old," he read. "Does your face itch?" The word itch had been underlined, and at the bottom, he saw the number 605.

He tore a hole in his pants he pulled them on so quickly. Before marching over he stopped to check out his door again. He couldn't find any damage.

The door to 605 shuddered from the force of his knocks. "Get the hell out here," he shouted.

Before leaving he'd grabbed a key to the apartment. When he inserted it into the knob, he couldn't get it to turn. He shook the knob, nearly broke the key off inside it. "I see how it is," he whispered, struck the door one last time. Halfway back to his apartment he glanced over his shoulder and saw the fingers at the blinds pulling back.

***

Hector helped him install new locks a few hours later. The people had clearly changed their own lock, and Roy had never bothered to alter his since buying the place. Maybe they'd been given, or stolen, a key from the previous owner.

"Decided to check in on something," Hector told him afterwards and pulled a crumpled piece of paper from his back pocket. Roy unfolded it to see the picture of what looked like a man in his early twenties. The newspaper article told him the man had gone missing.

"I saw him enter that place about a week ago," Hector said, pointed at the picture. "Sort of found this on a whim."

"Christ, you think they're killing people?" Roy asked.

"Maybe, but look at where he was last seen." "That's three states over."

"Says he was last seen on the sixth, and I saw him walk in that apartment on the eighth. Said they couldn't find any sign of foul play, neither. He just left home and never came back."

Roy set the paper down and slumped back into his chair. "Wasn't forced into the apartment when you saw him, was he?"

"Nah, he just walked in on his own. Looked kind of nervous to me, you know, fidgeting and stuff."

"Drug addict?"

"Different than that. Seen plenty of the people coming to score around here. No, he looked more…I don't know, higher class than that, out of his element. That kind of nervous."

Hector put his hands on the edge of the desk and leaned in closer to Roy. "I know you need to show your tough to keep a lot of these people in line, but given what you've told me about these freaks, just call the cops." He tapped the newspaper clipping. "Here's a pretty damn good reason to."

"I'll think about it."

Both men knew Roy wouldn't, and Roy didn't like the way Hector looked back at him before leaving the apartment, like he was staring at a doomed man.

"I'm not going to be scared out of my own god damn complex," he growled. Thing that bothered him most about the idea of calling the cops was that he might never know what was going on in that apartment.

***

Hunkering down around the side of the building annoyed Roy for the simple fact that he had to do it. From around the corner, he could just make out the door to 605, but anyone walking up to it wouldn't be able to see him.

Given the darkness he couldn't see the woman's face, though he thought she was older, something about her walk suggesting it. He began inching around the corner as she reached the door. Before entering she hesitated, hands cupped close to her chest, then reaching out and opening up the door.

She didn't knock, however, simply opening it, and Roy smiled at that as he hurried towards the front of the apartment.

Years had passed since the last time he fired the gun he pulled from his waistband. The knob turned easily in his grasp, let him crack the door slowly open, inhale the foul smell, and slip inside.

When the door first closed, he couldn't see much of anything. Somewhere deeper in the apartment a small light did flicker, and people were softly talking to each other, voices too low to be understood.

The smell burned Roy's nostrils, made bile rise in his throat, eyes practically watering from it, aware all the same that he recognized that smell from somewhere.

The walls caught the attention of his adjusting eyesight. He cocked his head, trying to make them out, to understand what he saw. He had to rise and move closer to it, finger gripping firmly down on the gun, the smell growing worse the closer he got. His stomach began contracting before he mentally grasped what he was looking at. The faces, hundreds of them in all, blended together, preventing him from understanding what they were until he got close enough to stare directly into one.

Someone had cut the faces off all these people, then sewn them together, a few tufts of hair even visible at the top of the skin. The oldest of them barely resembled what they had once been, the flesh rotted into nothing, while near the base of the wall, Roy could see the freshest of the bunch, the sewn corners still visibly encrusted with dried blood.

Leave, his mind told him, before they understood what he had seen. Go to the police and end this. Too many questions kept him from doing so.

A hallway up ahead curved to the left. Roy brought up the gun, prepared to shoot anything he saw as he rounded the corner and stared down the long hall. On the left he saw the open door and the soft light pouring out of it. He heard too a sound he couldn't place, chose not to try to place as he inched further across the carpeted floor, up to the open doorway, and peered inside. In the middle of the room a chair had been bolted to the floor, almost like a dentist's chair, and inside it he saw the woman. Beside her a large, muscular man stood with his back to Roy, leaning over her, a blade in his hand slowly cutting into the side of her face. The task was nearly complete, the blade cutting along the lower edge of her chin, a bloody line encircling her face. The man set down the wet blade and grabbed hold of her flesh, started pulling it back, tearing it from her body, until he revealed another face beneath the surface.

She had a larger mouth now, one stretching nearly to her ears, and her eyes were twice as big, encompassing the majority of her forehead. Where her nose had been a hole existed lined with brown covered skin.

Frozen, staring at the scene, Roy saw her head tilt towards him, massive eyes narrowing. The man followed her gaze, his own face nearly identical to hers, grotesque eyes latching onto Roy.

Before Roy could bring up the gun he heard the movement from his left. He saw a blur of skin a second before something hard cracked across the side of his head. The gun fired into the wall when Roy struck the floor, eyes watery, consciousness slipping away. He could see the man who had first opened the door to him kneeling down, his face more clearly like a mask of skin.

Roy's arm shook as he tried to bring up the gun. He saw the anger flash through the man's eyes, but not the stoic, false face, and before the gun could aim the man pulled his fist back, and sent Roy tumbling into darkness.

***

The pain woke him. His eyes snapped open, saw the deformed face hunched over him, working intently, a blade gripped in the large man's fingers. Straps prevented Roy from moving his head, but he still struggled, made the blade pierce deeper into the muscles on his face, and force the large man to pull back.

"He's awake," the man yelled.

"What the fuck are you people?"

The large man didn't answer, pulling away from the chair instead. A level of decay touched the room, the wallpaper dirty and peeling from the walls, the carpet strained dark brown and red. A light nearly blinded him, pulled down to just above his face.

A mask of skin still covered the other man's face when he walked into the room and bent over Roy, blocking out the light, turning his face into a black silhouette.

"He was struggling," the large man said.

"We're here to help you," the other man said, his voice muffled by the rotting lips covering his mouth.

"I don't need your fucking help," Roy shouted, tried vainly to tear through the thick leather straps holding him down.

"Maybe not, but we have to at least try. We've come to enjoy this location and would like to stay if at all possible." As he spoke he grabbed a syringe from a nearby table. "Given your age, you might be one of us. The ages have always been sporadic, but there is a pattern we've found, and you've given us no choice but to inspect you by force."

"Don't tear off my face," Roy pleaded.

"If you are one of us, you'll soon understand how liberating it is to add your false flesh to the others on the wall, and finally be free." He stabbed the needle into Roy's arm. The numbness spread quickly through his body, made his eyelids heavy, his muscles rubbery. The last sight Roy saw was the large man moving forward, the bloody blade still in his hand.

***

The second time around consciousness came slower to Roy. Every part of him felt terrible, and his first thoughts drifted towards a night of drinking, but his face felt too odd, too numb. He crawled from his bed and into the bathroom, blinded by the light, squinting when he leaned closer to the mirror.

He saw the writing before he saw his actual face. You're Not One of Us the message read.

In the mirror he saw the wet spit running down his numb lips, the poorly done stitches outlining his face. He tried to move his lips, felt them twitch.

Roy lurched from the bathroom, still dressed from the night before as he clawed open his front door and hurried down the steps. The door to apartment 605 stood ajar, the blinds up, and even before he reached it he could see the smooth interior, void of furniture.

A thick odor hung in the apartment, but the skin was gone, even the carpet pulled up. Two rusted bolts were all he found in the room he'd been held captive in. Four holes were drilled through the floor where the chair had been. Up above he saw the exposed wires coming down from the ceiling, no longer connected to an adjustable light.

He found the real damage in the back bedroom where the floor had been torn open. Through the large hole he saw a makeshift ladder. He descended into the cement portion of an underground sewer system for the city. Two large pipes greeted him, the only sounds from the water dripping through them. Was this where they had all been going, Roy asked himself? Roy suspected if he traveled far enough that he'd find something, but the throbbing in his face stopped him from taking a single step forward. They'd let him live once already.

As he pulled himself back into the bedroom, he heard the sound of the front door opening, followed by the hesitant voice calling out, "Hello?" The middle-aged man standing in the living room recoiled when Roy rounded the corner. He caught the man in the stomach before he could even move, dropping him to his knees, but only briefly, Roy immediately pulling him up, slamming him into the wall. "Who are you?" Roy breathed out.

"My name is Weldon Kehler," he said.

"What are you doing here?"

"I-I was told I could get help." Tears began to trickle down his cheeks, and looking closely at the man's eyes, Roy thought he could see something strange in them. "I'm not sure what I am."

The rage he'd felt when strapped to the chair made him throw the man to the floor and start hitting him. He didn't stop until the man's cheek had torn open and Roy thought he could see another mouth through the bloody rip in the skin.

Weldon held his hands close to his face when Roy finally pulled himself together and rose. "Get out of here," Roy said, and the man did, scrambling to his feet and out the door before Roy could reconsider.

The numbness had already begun to depart, and in its place came a sharp, fierce pain. He closed the door to apartment 605 behind him when he walked back to his home with all of the answers he had wanted.

The End.

Case File: #22047

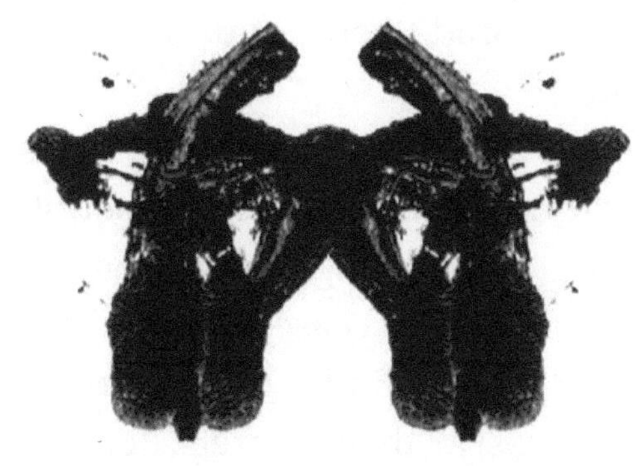

Chapelure by W. B. Stickel

According to the crew log little had happened since Jensen had last been on shift. A hard reboot of one of the data link processors, a password reset, and that was it.

Glad it wasn't busy—he hadn't slept well again and wasn't in the mood for any heavy thinking—Jensen clicked out of the crew log program and moved to the computer room's primary maintenance console. Waiting for him there was his night shift counterpart, a scraggly old Master Sergeant named Walker.

"Doing overnights now?" Jensen asked, knowing Walker normally worked the three-to-eleven shift.

Walker shrugged. "A hole in the schedule needed filling." Jensen nodded his cue-ball head. With funding constantly being rechanneled to the war effort, manpower issues had become a way of life for everyone across the military spectrum. "Looks like a slow night from the log."

"All quiet in the East," Walker replied, referring the eastern half of the United States, whose skies their unit, the Eastern Defense Sector, monitored twenty-four-seven.

"Quiet is good."

Walker stood, stretched, and idly slipped his hands into his pockets—a big no-no while in uniform. Jensen started to tell him to remove them, but a flickering of the room's lights stilled his tongue. When the flickering ceased, Walker was different: his body bloodied and burnt, limbs misshapen or missing, eyes floating like dead orbs in their sockets. Jensen flinched at the sight and backed away.

"You okay there, Jimmy?" Walker said, ribcage exposed. The lights flickered again, and everything returned to normal. Before Jenson could respond, Walker's partner for the late shift, Lou Smiley, popped up from behind one of the huge processing units. "Sanderson here yet?" he asked. Smiley was tall and lanky, in his mid-twenties, and looked uncannily like Dolph Lundgren's soviet boxer in Rocky IV.

"Haven't seen him," Jenson managed to say.

Walker gave Jensen the old fish eye, then grabbed his Gortex from the coat rack. He was in the middle of pulling it on when the door to the computer room opened and Sanderson came floundering through. "Sorry, sorry, everybody," the young two-striper said, apologizing as if he'd shown up late, when in fact he still had two minutes until he was officially on duty.

He plopped into a seat at the secondary maintenance console, which sat in the center of the room, and lay his buzzed head on the black table top.

Smiley plucked his parka off the back of Sanderson's chair. "Rough night, dude?"

Sanderson grunted and grabbed his crotch. "I'll say."

"Legal, I hope."

"Just barely."

Smiley snickered and crossed the room of whirring computer equipment. "Later," he said, making his exit. Just prior to the door closing, Jensen thought he saw something metallic and red jutting from the back of the man's head. A second later the door shut and both Smiley and the image were gone.

Jensen scowled, rubbed his eyes, and wondered what the hell was wrong with him.

"Sergeant Jensen," Walker said, heading for the door, "the reigns are all yours." Reaching the door he paused and snapped his fingers. "Oh, right. Wanted to show you something." He indicated the back left corner of the room and headed that way. Jensen, still scowling, followed.

They convened at the rear of an equipment rack that housed a complex if archaic recording system.

"Out of sheer boredom," said Walker, "last night me and Smiley started straightening out the cables back here. Figured we'd get them tidy, label what needed labeling, et cetera, et cetera. A royal pain in the ass but we got it done."

Somehow Jensen managed to set aside his dismay over what he'd just seen long enough to focus on what his counterpart was saying. He looked and was actually impressed by their handiwork. The two men had brought order to what had been a rat's nest of network and serial cables.

Walker took a knee and motioned toward the bottom of the rack, where an assortment of data cables, now tamed, flowed up from a hole cut in the raised floor. "We got everything figured out except . . . ." He jammed his hand down into the hole, extracted a skinny green cable, and showed it to Jensen. "Found this just lying beneath the floor. It's got an RJ45 on it but it's not labeled. The analyzer says it's connected to something, we just don't know what. The readings kept coming back with different numbers. We started to trace it out but couldn't find the other end."

"Hmm." Jensen studied the cable. Its green sheathing looked new.

"It goes under the floor, zig-zags through the cable trays, then goes up the wall over there," Walker pointed to the wall opposite them, "and heads up into the Catwalk." The Catwalk was the expansive maintenance level that loomed above most of the facility's work centers. "After buzzing about the trays up there, it heads over to the frame room, and buries itself under a heap of other Cat-5's. We followed it that far, then gave up."

"Show me."

If the computer room was brains of the Sector's mission, the frame room was the heart. All communications going to and leaving the building went through it; radar feeds, phone lines, fractional T1s, the whole kit and caboodle.

Gaining entrance via a palm scan and key code, Walker led Jensen down the first row of equipment on the left, and stopped about halfway, where a short wooden ladder stood. He pointed up at the cable tray suspended above. Standing out amongst its spaghetti-work cargo was a green Cat-5. The cable arced out from the flowing mass like a tea cup handle and was affixed with a label bearing a "trace this way" arrow.

Jensen assured Walker he'd figure it out, and with that, the two men parted ways.

***

Sanderson sat upright when Jensen reentered the computer room. "What's up, boss?"

Jensen told him, then went to his rucksack and retrieved his coffee thermos.

Sanderson groaned. "Give me a minute and I'll take care of it."

Jensen unscrewed the thermos' lid. "Nah. You're in no shape to be climbing ladders. I'll do it."

Another flickering of the lights swept the room. When it ceased, Sanderson's face was gone, replaced by a charred death mask. Jensen blinked and noticed it wasn't just his face that was gone but his whole front side, flayed to the bone and blackened like some bizarre Cajun delicacy.

As with the two prior instances, the lights flickered again and the normal Sanderson reappeared, fully intact. "Fun's all yours then, sir," the kid said.

Jensen did his best to hide his alarm and hastened back to his rucksack to collect himself. It had to be lack of sleep, he reasoned. His insomnia finally catching up, spawning weird visions. In a way, he supposed he should have expected something like this. The mind didn't function well without sufficient rest, and of late—since Michelle had left, taking Jamie with her— he'd only been sleeping two to three hours a night.

Praying that was all it was, Jensen downed his coffee, procured a set of wire cutters from the toolkit and headed for the door.

***

The wooden stepladder groaned under Jensen's weight.

"Yeah, yeah," he said, setting to work after the cable. "I could stand to lose a few pounds. So what."

Once he got started, it didn't take him long to figure out why Walker and Smiley had given up on the thing where they had. In addition to being buried deep within the tangled mass of cables running through the tray, it had been run it the most absurd manner: looping in pointless circles, slithering this way and that, going everywhere and nowhere at once, it seemed. Because of this, it took him close to an hour to decipher where it went, and even then what he found didn't make much sense. After its grand tour of the room, it left the trays running along the far wall and scurried up to a hole cut in one of the ceiling's tiles—back, incredibly, into the Catwalk.

"Christ," Jensen said, wanting to punch whichever dipshit had run it that way. Shaking his head, he got down off the ladder and returned to the computer room.

Sanderson chuckled when Jensen told him what he'd found. "That's bananas. So, what now?"

"I guess I head up into the Catwalk."

Sanderson nodded, then smirked.

"What?" Jensen asked.

"You, uh, gonna do a little dance up there?"

Despite everything going on in his head, Jensen had to smile at that. A Right Said Fred reference from a twenty-something year old. Not bad. "You know me," he replied. "So sexy it hurts."

***

The Catwalk had various access points scattered throughout the facility. Jensen typically preferred the one located in the Utilities plant, as it was closest to the computer room. His badge wasn't coded for the plant, so he had to buzz the technician on duty to let him in.

Staff Sergeant Burrell answered the door, face smeared with red grease. Jensen was surprised to see the man. Last he'd heard, Burrell had transferred out west.

"Thought you went to McChord," he said.

"Nah," Burrell replied, nodding to the giant generators behind him. "Stuck here, fixing these things. Like you're stuck fixing your computers."

Jensen explained why he was there, then negotiated the maze of power units, water pipes and air handlers that led back to the maintenance ladder. The ladder ascended to a small landing, at the end of which sat the porthole leading to the Catwalk. Jensen scaled the ladder and used his supervisor's key to access the porthole.

A chain of hanging lights automatically came on when he entered the Catwalk's main corridor, illuminating the steel-grate walkway that coursed through the entire maintenance level.

Securing the porthole, Jensen started along the corridor. To his left was a wide trough swimming with cables. To his right, a series of doors fitted with placards indicating which section they sat above: Server Room, Computer Room, Vault. Jensen halted at the one labeled Frame Room and used his key to gain entry. The lights within also came on by themselves, revealing a room comprised of a narrow strip of concrete beset on each side by the metal framework that held up the Frame Room's tiled ceiling.

"All right, you stupid cable," he said, looking around. "Where are— "

An abrupt burning sensation in his chest cut his words short. The burning flared beneath his sternum and rapidly branched out, ebbing through his veins and flowing into his extremities. Distantly wondering if this was what boiling blood felt like, Jensen lifted his hands, expecting them to catch fire. When he looked, though, the burning subsided, giving way to a more powerful sensation—a soul-moving euphoria that washed over him in waves and brought him teary-eyed to his knees.

A time passed then and he was overcome by thoughts of Michelle and Jamie. Their faces hovered in his mind and he kept thinking how wonderful things had been before they had left. What, he wondered darkly, had caused their estrangement? What in the world had gone so terribly wrong that would compel Michelle to flee and take Jamie with her? For the life of him he couldn't remember, and deep down he knew that he should.

"Michelle," he whispered. "Jamie."

Their names tumbled emptily from his lips, evaporating into the black-hole silence of the room. He went to speak them again, to give them a little more life, but before he could the murmuring started.

Engrossed as he was in the mystery of his family's collapse, Jensen at first barely registered the sound. But then the murmurs doubled in volume, and an invasive notion poked its way through his ruminations: who besides himself and Sanderson, and maybe Burrell, could have possibly had the need to come up into the Catwalk—on a Saturday no less—to make such a sound?

Jensen mulled it over and came up with nothing.

Eyebrows knitting into a V, he took a step forward and listened closer. Within the murmuring he detected two distinct intonations—one male, one female—though he couldn't make out what they were saying.

Still coming up with nothing, he resolved that it was probably just a couple of frisky airmen who'd snuck up here, no doubt with Burrell's help, in hopes of engaging in some "extracurricular activity". A risky thing to do while on duty but it wasn't unheard of.

Jensen had a mind to report them to Security Forces but promptly discarded the idea. Between all the inner turmoil he had going on and the unresolved task at hand, the less bullshit he had to deal with, the better.

"Okay," he groused, trying to push all thoughts unrelated to the pesky cable out of his head. "Let's just get this over with."

With great effort, he rechanneled his focus on the cable and resumed his search.

He found his quarry to the right of the concrete walkway, springing up from the hole he'd located down below. Tied-wrapped to a chain of support beams, it traveled up the wall, across the ceiling, and partway down the wall to the left, where it then disappeared into yet another hole.

Jensen's face became a mien of disbelief. "You've got to be shitting me." As if in response to this, the murmuring surged several more decibels.

Jensen glanced left, where it was coming from. Dots connected in his head and his face went slack. "Of course it's going where they are," he said. "Where else would it go?"

Guessing he was going to learn who his Catwalk companions were after all; Jensen vacated the room and went to the next door down. The murmuring was a tad louder there, though no more intelligible.

Curious if he'd catch them in a compromising position, he went to put his key into the door's lock but noticed there was no keyhole, just the door knob. As he stood there contemplating the oddness of this, a storm of butterflies fluttered in his belly, and a tingly sense of deja vu crept over him. He started to think Oh god, what now? when his eyes traveled up to the door's placard and saw the word printed on it.

Home.

The word seemed to catalyze something in him and next he knew fragments of the bad dream he'd had the night before—his recurring deployed-to-Afghanistan dream—flashed through his head: receiving orders to Bagram with several member from the unit; enduring the long flight over; in-processing; he and Sanderson getting assigned to base communications; the others being divvied up to their respective areas of expertise—logistics, security, operations.

A night three months after arriving; dining at the mess hall with all the troops from the unit; everyone in good spirits, enjoying their food and joking with British soldiers at the next table. The base sirens then going off; a voice coming over the loud speaker, commanding: "Cover! Cover! Cover!" Everyone in the mess hall grabbing their gear and diving under the tables; the frightening shriek of the Centurion anti-mortar arrays erupting along the base's interior fence line.

Sanderson yelling "Mortars!" excitedly like it was happening in a movie; the east side of the mess hall coming apart in a hail of fire and shrapnel. A second explosion, this one inside the mess hall, close, so close. A white-hot flash. Men screaming. Bodies everywhere.

The fragments ceased there.

Jensen shut his eyes. "Home," he said, and sensed the fabric of everything unraveling around him. He reached for the door knob, grasped it, and a lightning storm of firing synapses arced across his brain. He turned the knob, pushed the door open. He took a breath and stepped into a room that did not exist in the world that he knew.

***

A thin miasma filled the air.

Through it Jensen discerned vague shapes. Gradually the shapes came into focus, forming a scene he recognized. His bedroom at home. The way it had been before Michelle had left. Clean, tidy. Bed covers made. Pictures on the wall. A pleasant vanilla scent in the air.

For a moment, Jensen believed it really was his room. But when he looked closer he began to notice all the tiny flaws. The spacing of things, the colors, the textures. They added up fast and he realized it was a replica. He was pondering the possible reasons behind its being here when a gentle voice sounded behind him.

"Mr. Jensen?"

Jensen gave a start and whirled around, fists at the ready. A tall, slim man in his mid to late fifties was standing there, clipboard in his hands. He was dressed in a light blue dress shirt, black slacks and a paisley tie. He wore trendy, black-framed glasses, sported a thin mustache and had his hair parted neatly on the side.

"Who the hell are you?" Jensen demanded.

The man smiled. "You are aware of me, then?" he asked, a slight French lilt peppering his words. He stood where the bedroom's closet should have been, if this had actually been Jensen's bedroom. Instead of the closet there was but a lone exam table and next to that an open door leading to another room.

"Of course I'm aware of you," Jensen said. "Who are you?"

The man's smile broadened. He seemed very pleased about something. "Mr. Jensen, my name is Rene Linnet. Doctor, if you will. It is a great pleasure to meet you. The real you." He extended a hand, which Jensen ignored.

"Are we suppose know each other?" Jensen said.

"In a sense, yes." Linnet waited a few beats, then asked: "Mr. Jensen, where do you think we are?"

"What?"

"Is it your understanding that we are at the Eastern Defense Sector. In New York?"

"Where else would we be?"

Linnet dropped his hand. "Slightly more north than that, I'm afraid." He placed the clipboard on the exam table behind him. "Mr. Jensen, we have some very delicate things to discuss. Things that may not be easy for you to accept."

Jensen simply peered at the man, silent, processing.

The doctor continued. "First, you are not in New York. You are not even in the United States. You are on Greenly Island. In Quebec."

"Quebec, Canada?" Jensen sneered. "Bullshit."

Linnet gestured to the window on the opposite side of the room, near the replica bed. "See for yourself."

Jensen readily obliged. Beyond the window pane laid a small stretch of land dotted with rocks and trees and wisps of snow. Beyond that, the endless blue sea.

Linnet removed his glasses and rubbed his nose. "Please, look down at yourself, at your clothes."

Jensen turned from the window and looked. Instead of his military uniform he was decked out in a puke-green hospital gown that hung loosely from his thin frame. His heart flip-flopped in his chest. Incredulity ricocheted through him. Confused and angry, he advanced on Linnet and raised a fist. "What's going on? What the fuck is this?"

Fear glinted in Linnet's eyes but he held his ground. "No need for that, Mr. Jensen. Look, I was going to save this for a little later but perhaps . . ."

He turned, facing the door near the exam table. "You can come out now," he said.

There was a shuffling noise, then a woman in her late thirties appeared in the doorway. Behind her trailed a girl no older than fourteen. Both were both dressed in warm clothes, the elder in a brown turtleneck and slacks, the younger in a black hoodie and jeans. They seemed slightly older than Jensen recalled, but their beautiful faces and matching jet-black manes were unmistakable.

Michelle and Jamie.

***

Michelle's eyes lingered on Jensen momentarily before switching to Linnet.

"You were listening, yes?" the doctor asked her. "Yes," she said, lip trembling. "Are you sure he's—?" Linnet nodded cheerfully. "I'm sure."

Michelle released an exultant sob and pounced on Jensen, wrapping her arms around him. Her words came out in a weepy jumble. "Jim-oh-baby-I-thought-I-might-never-get-you-back!"

Then Jamie was on him, clinging tight, mascara-tears streaking her cheeks. "Dad!" she cried.

The fractured family embraced for two full minutes, the women crying, Jensen laboring frantically to comprehend what was going on. At last, they broke apart and Jensen saw his wife cast her gaze at the doctor.

Linnet picked up his clipboard and excused himself, claiming he needed a few minutes to inform his colleagues that Trial 67 had met with success.

Jensen crossed the replica bedroom and sat on the bed. His mind spun.

He peered at Michelle, his eyes begging for answers.

Michelle and Jaime joined him on the bed. "You came back," Michelle uttered, taking his hand. "The doctors at Landstuhl and Walter Reed—they said you never would, not the way you were. Dr. Linnet was the only one who gave you a chance."

Jensen touched his own face; it was stubbly with beard growth. "Maybe you should start from the beginning."

Michelle grasped his hand and did just that.

***

Afghanistan had been no dream. Jensen had actually gone; he'd in fact volunteered for the assignment, thinking the move would give him a leg up on the competition when the next promotion opportunity arose. Michelle hadn't liked it, as there were issues in their marriage that needed tending to, but supported him nonetheless. As she always had.

When the mess hall incident occurred, Michelle had nearly suffered a nervous breakdown. Someone had screwed up and she'd initially been told Jensen was among the dead. But then the official report came across listing Sanderson, Walker, Burrell and Smiley as deceased and Jensen as merely "injured". The military had apologized profusely for the mix up, but Michelle had told them to shove their apologies up their incompetent asses.

"To make matters worse," Michelle recounted, "they wouldn't let me fly to Landstuhl to see you. They made me wait until they transferred you to Walter Reed in Bethesda, a full week later. When I did finally get to see you, all I heard was 'persistent vegetative state'. And it was true. You were in bad shape, with minimal activity. No one had any hope. It was a nightmare."

Clueless what to do but refusing to give up on him, she decided to educate herself on his condition. She spent countless hours reading and researching and conferring with specialists, and became a quasi-expert on brain trauma. Which was great, except none of it really helped. Worse, each time she visited him, he seemed to have drifted a little further away.

With no other choice, she began to investigate experimental options, a path that eventually led her to Linnet's personal webpage. Intrigued by what she read; she arranged a meeting with him. After they talked, Linnet agreed to take Jensen on as a case, on the condition that Jensen be moved to an institution in Canada.

As for what the institution was, Michelle only knew what Linnet had told her: that it was the brainchild of a global group of neuro-specialists who wanted to build a center dedicated to new treatments for brain and spinal injuries. Its official designation was that of a research and development venture but much more went on within its walls. The division Linnet headed, for example, dealt exclusively with experimental approaches to waking coma victims—most of which were off the books.

"He used to be a neurosurgeon in the Royal Canadian Air Force," Michelle said, "and he has a soft spot for injured vets."

Linnet returned from conferring with his colleagues then. He sat in a chair by the bed and got caught up on what Michelle had already revealed. "Yes" he added, "this is a state-of-the-art facility which the Canadian government mostly ignores, for now. It is a big place with many patients from all over the world. We do not discriminate. We even have Taliban here. Does any of this bother you?"

Given all that he had just heard, and considering that he'd just gotten his life back, Jensen didn't care in the least. "I just want to know what you did to me."

Linnet brightened at the inquiry and relayed how, over the course of a year, he'd tried numerous concoctions of neuron-stimulants without success, until Trial 41 reaped significant results. "It woke you but you were not here. Your brain, it seemed, had locked onto an average day before your deployment and you physically went about a modified version of that day— and kept doing it. It was most fascinating."

Jensen brooded on this. "So, I've been going around all this time re-enacting some boring day in my life? Doing, like, everything here that I thought I was doing in my head?"

"Yes," Linnet confirmed. "It was quite awkward at first, with your atrophied limbs. But the staff helped out until you could walk unassisted, then you were on your own. You were monitored throughout but we allowed you to wander the building as your mind saw fit. Nothing to be embarrassed about either. When you needed to use the restroom, you went into an actual restroom."

Jensen stared out the window. "Holy shit."

Linnet chuckled. "A great accomplishment, yes, but I was not fully satisfied because you were still stuck in the past. So we tried some newer treatments. What I'm going to call my 'Chapelure' variants."

"Chapelure?"

"Breadcrumbs, in French," Linnet clarified. "Dopamine-based stimuli designed to show your brain the way home, so to speak. The first few runs had encouraging effects. We immediately saw your routine change. Whereas before you kept cycling through a day without much required of you, all at once you began trying to find things. Your keys, a lost book, then, at last, some kind of cable. This cable—it became a manifestation of the Chapelure. The alterations I made in Trial 67 seemed to finally do the trick."

A dozen or so other doctors came into the room then, wide-eyed and happy-faced.

"Ah, yes," Linnet said. "Come to see the proof." He looked at Jensen. "If you're up to it, you mind speaking with them for a short time?"

Jensen glanced at the ceiling again, then at his wife and daughter, who both nodded as if to say it was okay. Overwhelmed, yet filled with cloud-nine gratitude, Jensen agreed and watched as the crowd of neuro-specialists moved in around him like zombies at a human buffet.

***

The question-and-answer session lasted a good half-hour before Linnet finally shooed his colleagues away. He departed with them, ensuring the Jensen clan that when he returned, they'd discuss what lay ahead.

Michelle excused herself to use the restroom, while Jamie stretched and gravitated to the window to admire the view.

Jensen remained on the bed, pondering a great many things. It was all so much to digest. He had about a billion more questions to ask concerning everything: the institution, his military status, where he and Michelle stood, how Michelle had managed to do everything she'd done, how Jamie was doing, how long he'd been in the coma, why no one else had seemed to notice what lingered on the ceiling above the bed . . .

Jensen stood and joined his daughter at the window. She leaned against him, put her head on his shoulder, something she hadn't done since she was child. In the distance, the ocean waters glittered madly under the fading sun. Jensen smiled and tried as hard as he could not to think about the green cable running across the ceiling.

The End.

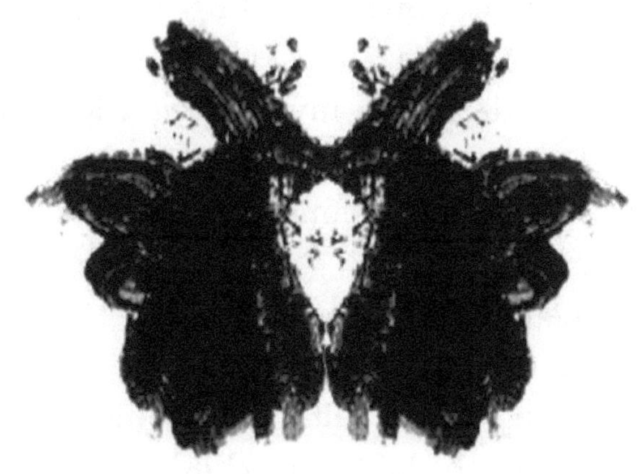

Eyes Like Rivers by Anthony Camarillo

Jerry crouched with his back firmly pressed against the base of the steel fryers that lined the western wall of Speedy Burger's kitchen. The freshly painted white walls and ceiling, coupled with the luminous chrome utilities neatly packed into the small confines of the hamburger stand were an ironic contrast to the darkness of Jerry's predicament. He held on to the protruding, red-rubber handle of one of the fry baskets above his head, as if for security, but the beads of sweat inching their way down the sides of his forehead were red flags giving away the unease that weighed heavily upon him.

Why the hell did I have to say yes, he wondered while his thoughts rushed throughout his brain like rapids, one horrific possibility converging with the next.

Jerry rarely worked the closing hours at Speedy Burger and whenever he was asked to cover for someone's night shift, he usually turned them down, spurting out the first lie that presented itself in his head.

Sorry, I have a date with my girlfriend tonight. Sorry, my grandmother is sick at home and she needs me to serve her dinner. Sorry, midterms are coming up and a good study session has been calling my name.

The fact of the matter was he really didn't like being out late at night anymore, especially after what had happened to him the year before. It wasn't that he felt that he couldn't protect himself from strangers or that he had some childish fear of the dark, for Christ's sake, he was a twenty-two-year-old adult, not to mention he was just shy of six feet in height. No, what bothered Jerry was the horrid thing he had done fourteen months ago.

It all happened in mid-October, a few days after Jerry's twenty-first birthday, during the night of his sixth straight night of heavy drinking. Someone might have called it the early stages of alcoholism, but no, Jerry was no alcoholic, he just couldn't resist the occasional seven, eight, shit, maybe even nine shots of whiskey a night. Hell, he had waited twenty-one long years to be able to do the damn thing legally, so in a way, he had earned it. Besides, what was the worst that could happen? A hangover?

But Jerry learned the harsh reality of alcohol's succubus-nature the hard way. The visor of innocence that had shielded his eyes for years was finally removed on that foggy, October night. He could recall the memory like a freshly captured Polaroid photo, hazy and undeveloped at first, but with time the image would be as vivid as a scene frozen in action. He could barely distinguish where the right side of his lane ended and the parallel sidewalk began through his drunken eyes. It still haunted his dreams; behind the bleak darkness of his eyelids, he could see his 2001 Ford-150 slamming through that young, petite girl like a bulldozer going head-to-head with a scarecrow. He was oblivious until his windshield was cracked and streaked with blood to match his truck's paintjob.

Since then, he detested the idea to be on the road after sunset and did all he could to avoid it whenever possible. If it hadn't been for the fact that his brother, Eddie, was a mechanic that specialized in body-repair, he probably wouldn't have been able to drive at all after that night, let alone walk the streets as a free man. Yeah, maybe Eddie was somewhat of a good luck charm to Jerry, but not nearly as lucky as the charm he picked up that horrible night in October. Yeah, that's what really saved his ass.

When he'd hit her, he didn't really know what he should do. Her body was sprawled out lifelessly beside the road, leaking dark streams of blood into the lush, green grass. He stared at the corpse with the distant interest of a person put under the trance of a hypnotist, seeing the horror in front of his eyes but not quite registering it. The blue bracelet was yards away from her but casually perched up on a pile of yellow leaves. He walked over to it and picked it up. There were six blue beads on it, strung together with a band made of white and blue threads. The beads each had their own character on it, spelling out: Rovers, only instead of the letter "o", there was an image of an eye. He thought that maybe the eye could have also stood for the letter "i", but he wasn't quite sure. Rivers makes more sense, he thought to himself. He didn't know why it made more sense to him; it just did.

Jerry now looked down at his left arm that was wrapped around his knees and the same bracelet that was currently on his wrist. The eyeball stared at him and he exhaled with a feeling of calm.

You'll get through this, Jerry, just chill out, he told himself. Since he had held on to that bracelet and worn it daily, he somehow managed to have the best luck, no matter what the odds were. His grades had been better than ever, he had acquired two raises within six months of work and he never left Las Vegas without more money than he had traveled there with. Besides, if he hadn't been caught for a drunk hit-and-run over a year after the incident, what was the worst that could happen to him now?

He raised his head a bit and stared out the north drive-through window that faced the main highway. Still, not a soul roamed the streets. It was well past midnight and most of the homes across the street were filled with sleeping people, resting for Monday morning. The entire street was closed off from the traffic light on the western side of Speedy to the other traffic light on the eastern edge of the property for construction. Not a single car had crossed in front of the hamburger stand that whole weekend. Today was a special day though because the weather forecast had predicted rain causing the construction workers to delay the concrete pouring until tomorrow morning. Speedy Burger and the highway that stood guard in front of it were a ghost town.

The only reason Jerry was stuck working a Sunday closing shift in the confining white walls of Speedy's kitchen was because he heard that a different worker from the Speedy Burger in Ventura would be coming down to help fill in and also because he simply couldn't think of a good excuse to worm his way out of the responsibility. His manager came down with the flu and the other guy who was supposed to work the closing shift was fired days before for stealing money during other closing shifts. Nobody else was available to close on that Sunday night so he gave in and decided he would just have to get through it. How bad could this night possibly go, he had thought to himself on his way to work earlier that day, not realizing that he was walking blindfolded into a lion's den.

***

From the moment Jerry walked into the backroom to clock in at Speedy's, Carl, the transfer, gave him the strangest looks. He stared at Jerry with those cold, piercing blue eyes, his irises rolling up and down as if scanning him, trying to evaluate whether or not he posed a threat. Jerry couldn't stand people like that, staring at him as if already accusing him of something he didn't do. Perhaps it was the paranoia that never fully dissipated, but lingered like a shadow, even though he was never so much as suspected for the death of the little mystery girl.

"So, what's your name, son?" Jerry's skin crawled. He couldn't stand anyone besides his father calling him that. Carl didn't look much older than fifty years of age, more or less the same height as Jerry and outweighed him by at least fifty pounds. Sure, it was possible that he might be old enough to be his father, but their age difference wasn't what got to Jerry, it was the respect issue. Even if the guy had been three times his size, he wasn't going to take that condescending shit from him.

"I'm Jerry, how about you, son?" Carl's eyes did that same surveying motion, scrutinizing Jerry. Didn't like that one did you, old man?

"The name's Carl. I'll see you inside the kitchen," Carl murmured and then looked down at his clipboard before muttering, "son."

The rest of the night trudged on with a dreadful slowness. He usually had more fun on nights when he stayed home to write papers analyzing British poetry from the 1700's. The only customers that appeared at the walk-up window were those that were willing to park a block away in either direction of the hamburger stand and walk the rest of the way. The dual drive-through lanes on either side of the kitchen were vacant for the whole night, only adding to the stuffy, uneasy atmosphere.

Jerry and Carl remained silent the whole night, speaking to each other only when they needed something from the opposite side of the kitchen or when Carl would ask (or maybe "tell" was a better word for it) Jerry to retrieve something from the backroom. The night dragged but Jerry was thankful for the lack of confrontation. Jerry might not have been one to take shit from someone verbally, but when it came down to actually making a stand, he would do what most cowards do, back down.

"So… where did you get that watch, Jerry?"

Jerry had been so used to the quiet that the question threw him off. He had to pause and look up from his repetitious, potato-dicing hands to realize he was being asked a question.

"Watch? You mean this bracelet?"

"Oh, I couldn't tell from over here… it's just a bracelet?"

"Yeah, look it says 'rivers'," Jerry held his arm up to Carl as he read it aloud. Carl shot a glance at Jerry's wrist and then pulled his eyes back to the spatula in his hand, flipping the lone patty that sizzled on the grill.

"That's a nice bracelet… weird that it has an eye where the 'i' should be," Carl commented, not lifting his eyes from the grill.

Jerry didn't speak.

"Where'd you get it?"

Jerry looked up to see that Carl was staring directly at him, his eyes as piercing as ever, locked on to his own eyes as if peering into his soul.

"I—I got it from a girl I used to know…" Jerry lied and looked away from Carl, hoping his eyes didn't give him away.

"Hmm… what does the eye mean?"

"I don't really remember, she told me a long time ago," Jerry lied once more, resisting Carl's hypnotic glare.

"Oh. Well, that's pretty cool Jerry. Hey, so how about you go take your last ten-minute break and then when you come back, I'll take mine? Sound good?"

Jerry nodded.

"Well then… see you in ten," Carl smiled and switched back to the sizzling meat on the grill.

***

Jerry took one last, long drag from the Camel Crush that drooped from his lips and then flicked the butt end into the highway. The small ember that burned inside the remaining tobacco fizzled out, dying like any hope of seeing Monday morning that might have once been lounging in the back of Jerry's mind. The burning red eye extinguished itself completely as Jerry made his way back towards the kitchen, noticing that the floodlights that protruded from each roof corner of the rectangular shaped building that served as the backroom of Speedy Burgers were turned off. He pulled his phone out of his pocket, noting the time. 12:40. Even as slow as business had been that night, Jerry knew it was too early to start closing up the restaurant just yet. Lisa is going to have a lot to hear about Carl, Jerry thought to himself as he could already imagine relaying how bad of a manager the transfer was to his current manager.

"Alright Carl, you can go ahead and—" Jerry stopped midsentence as he opened the door, finding the kitchen completely empty. What the hell?

"Carl!" He yelled out each window but the only response he was given were the slight rasps of dried out leaves making their way across the pavement of the empty lot. The PA system, he thought, switching his eyes to the black microphone that hung near the register at the walk-up window.

43

"Carl, I'm back from my break," Jerry's voice boomed throughout the property, "If you're around, you can go ahead and take your break. I'll run the ship from here." With that, he set the microphone back in its place and then turned back to the grill.

Damn, that Carl is one creepy son-of-a-bitch, he commented in his own mind, trying not to remind himself that he was the murdering son-of-a-bitch here. Carl was just a transfer, someone he wouldn't have to see ever again, as long as he didn't take any trips to the Speedy Burger in Ventura. Tomorrow morning he would laugh about all of this and wonder how any manager could be as irresponsible as Carl.

But maybe I should try one more time.

Jerry looked back at the microphone. It was as if he was a magnet and that microphone was an opposite charge, inevitably drawing him back. He picked it up once more.

"Carl?" But this time his voice didn't boom; it was nothing more than a whisper to an empty room. The PA system had been shut off somehow. What the fuck, man!

He could feel a chill inch its way down his spine, allowing the hairs on his forearms to stand at attention. Alright, think rationally, Jerry. The lights went out and now the PA, it must be some sort of electrical bullshit; that maintenance guy never gets it right anyway. That damned Romanian always had more of an interest in telling me how to avoid a head cold than actually fix the wiring in this older-than-hell building. What was his name… George?

Jerry was so lost in his own thoughts that he failed to realize the lights inside the kitchen flutter, but his attention was held with a firm grasp once the fryers and the grill turned off with the abruptness of a flipped switch.

This asshole has to be playing some kind of joke, he thought to himself. With the anger bubbling underneath his skin, flushing his face red with such an alarming realization, he grabbed the kitchen door handle and yanked it open.

"Don't move another inch."

Jerry stopped in his tracks, pausing to hear more from the distant voice like he had plenty of times before, sneaking into his house late at night, hoping not to awaken his parents.

"Step back into the kitchen," the voice commanded, "and lock the door. You're not going to leave right now, and if you want to leave at all, you'll do as I say."

Jerry didn't have to see his face to know that the voice was coming from Carl. He hadn't known the middle-aged man yet for more than a few hours but there was no mistaking it. Each word that spewed from Carl's mouth was direct and cutting, just like the eyes that sat eagerly in his head.

Jerry couldn't see where Carl was commanding him from but the voice felt close; perhaps Carl was standing on the opposite side of the kitchen wall but Jerry had no desire to test his luck. From that moment and onward, Jerry crouched against the cool, steel fryers, hoping that a hungry policeman would wander onto Speedy's property, believing it to be open until 2 a.m. instead of 1 a.m., but the situation never occurred.

Minutes passed, an hour passed, then two, and finally it was a little after three in the morning. Jerry's legs were stiff from kneeling in the same position until finally he stood up, his joints crackling as he straightened himself. As he rose from his position of safety, the lights flickered back on and the oil in the fryer began bubbling with life. He heard a door shut and as his head swiveled on his neck, he realized what was at the furthest window of the kitchen. Jerry lurched back and almost lost his balance, not believing what he was seeing.

"Open the door," Carl spoke, with a long rifle pointed at Jerry's head through the open window, from the other side of the door. Jerry knew he had to react but the situation left him dumbfounded, unable to move. He was an animal opposed by headlights.

"Look, Jerry. Either you open the door and maybe live to see tomorrow, or you can stand there with that ridiculous look on your face and wear it to your funeral. It's your choice."

Jerry took his time approaching the door, moving his feet with a slow stride similar to that of a heavy man making his way through thigh-high water. Who is this man, Jerry let the question make its way across his mind, unanswered.

Jerry unlocked the door and took a step back, allowing Carl to make his way into the kitchen. Jerry realized the irony at once, letting in an armed man with open arms. He had to hold his breath before his dark humor allowed a chuckle to make its way through his teeth.

"Down on your knees," Carl muttered, his eyes still fierce as two blue flames.

"I don't remember there being a rifle in the backroom, I must have missed it when I clocked in."

"Lucky for me, I went to the range before work tonight and something in my gut told me it'd be best to keep it in the back of my truck. God has a strange way of putting people in the right situations at just the right time, doesn't He?"

"If you came in here to shoot me down, why did you wait so long?" Jerry asked as he slowly knelt down, making sure to keep his movements calm and contained, as to avoid from startling Carl's trigger finger. Instead of answering the words, Carl answered once again with that rapid movement of the eyes. Those evil, hate-filled eyes.

Jerry's skin crawled as he felt Carl's gaze move up and down his body, those cold eyes flowing over him like rivers. Like rivers.

Jerry looked down at his own wrist, to the exact spot that Carl's eyes had come to rest at. Rivers. He read the blue beads once more… Rivers.

"Why did I wait?" Carl replied but Jerry's mouth remained closed.

"I wanted you to suffer, just as you let my daughter suffer. I wanted you to die inside, just like you let my daughter die."

Jerry let those words resonate inside him. He looked again at the bracelet, his bracelet, but he knew it wasn't truly his. What he thought at first to be a good luck charm, was actually an omen, a warning of the end that would eventually catch up to him.

"I know we just met, but I realize I left something out, something I should have told you to begin with. My name is Carl, Carl Rivers. And you, Jerry, murdered my daughter, Samantha Rivers. I gave that bracelet to my daughter at least six years ago and now you, like the scum that you are, wear it like a trophy, boasting the fact that you killed a twelve-year-old girl.

Tell me how you feel about this, Jerry. Tell me what it feels like to be a murderer."

Jerry tried to utter an apology or some sort of explanation but his throat felt clogged and the inside of his mouth felt like it was lined with cotton.

"Lay on your back, Jerry."

Jerry hesitated and began to reverse when Carl advanced on him, shoved him in the chest causing him to lose his balance. As he fell backwards, a bright light flashed before his eyes, two loud shots went off and a burst of pain shot throughout his whole body. It felt as if his legs had been set on fire and he was quite close in his guess. He looked down to see that Carl had shattered both of his kneecaps with a bullet in each. Crimson stained the chrome equipment and white walls that the kitchen comprised of. Carl set the rifle down and then picked up a pot from underneath the fryers, ignoring Jerry's screams and pleas for help. Jerry clawed at the ground around him but had no energy left in his muscles to pull himself in any direction.

"I know what you're thinking, Jerry. 'How is this psychopath going to clean up this mess before tomorrow morning?' Well, lucky for the both of us, my first job as a teenager was with a cleaning service. I have a feeling this kitchen is going to look cleaner than it has ever looked before."

The sides of Carl's mouth turned upwards and surfaced one of the most diabolical of smiles, the smirk of a man serving the coldest plate of revenge, straight from the freezer.

"By the way, since you've probably been wondering for a long time now, I'll fill you in on something. That eye stood for me, Jerry. It way my way of letting Samantha know that I would always watch over her. I may be late, but I'm not going to let an opportunity go by if I can help it."

Carl reached into the fryer and scooped out the steel pot, filled almost to the brim with oil. Jerry's eyes filled with terror as he saw the steam still arising from the boiling hot oil. It may have been sitting still for a while, cooling, but oil takes quite a while to completely cool off. The burns on his forearms from previous fryer accidents were enough to remind him of this unfortunate fact.

"Anything left to say that you won't be able to tell me from hell?" As Jerry was about to answer, Carl tilted the pot and let the oil flow over him, submerging Jerry's head like a drowning man in a gushing river.

The End.

Case File: #24254

Last Pass by Miracle Austin

Decapitated head found.

FM 6969 claimed another victim, Michael discovered on the front page of the newspaper. His iPhone vibrated on the table in his dorm room.

"Speak."

"Michael, please come home," Wichita, his sister, cried out. "What's wrong?"

"It's Big Mama Rose. She had another heart attack."

He packed up and jumped into his cranberry Mustang with JD riding shotgun and a few of his friends secured in an ice-packed cooler behind his seat.

Driving up to Wraw, Texas, he thought about how Big Mama Rose raised him and his little sis after their mom left them watching *The Bugaloos* one Saturday morning.

She never returned.

In no time, he found himself pulling into the hospital parking lot and walking down the cold white halls to room 711.

Big Mama Rose looked like a shriveled-up dandelion, once so proud and strong.

"It's me. Michael." She opened her eyes and reached for his face but fell back onto the pillow. "My boy," she whispered, "I've been waiting for you."

"I rushed to get to you as soon as I could."

"Ssshhh. I know."

"I'm so sorry for being out of touch all this time. You forgive me?" Tears ran down his face, as he kneeled down on one knee next to her bedside.

"I did that a long time ago, son."

"Thank you. I don't deserve it."

"Nonsense. Give me a sugar."

He kissed her cheek, making sure he didn't disturb her oxygen headgear.

"Can I get you something?"

"No, I have all I need now—you. I know all about your troubles, DWIs, and arrest."

"I shouldn't be surprised since Wichita loves to run her fat trap!" A dozen frown wrinkles popped out on his forehead, as he stared down at the polished floor.

"Look, I don't want to see you end up with a bowl of regrets. It's time for you to change, son. I want to share something with you." "Mama Rose, you need your rest," he said, looking up at her.

"No, I don't."

Using all the strength she possessed, she pushed the button on her bed's remote control to raise herself up.

"I came here to see about you, not for one of your stories."

"You, sit down right there. You need to hear this."

"All right."

He stood up and walked over to the flimsy plastic chair in the corner.

He dragged it to her bedside and sat down in front of her.

"It was October 31, 1942, 100 degrees, a record scorcher for Halloween. My older brother Coop planned on proposing to Madison, his high school steady. She could've passed for Dorothy Dandridge's double."

"You told me that Coop never married, enlisted in the army, and later died in combat." "I know."

"Why is this so important for you to tell me now? You need to rest, not talk."

"I don't have much time left. I need you to just listen to what I have to tell you."

The hospital gown swallowed her worn body.

"I really wish you would listen to me for a change," he said, but it was as though she didn't hear him.

"Now, where was I? Oh... Coop worked three jobs that summer and sold his red Ford truck, so he could get her an engagement ring from a fancy mail order catalog in New York. Madison drove up FM 6969 to meet him at the lake."

Mama Rose coughed several times, and Michael stood up to stroke her warm skeletal back.

"See, you need to rest. You're pushing yourself too much for something that's not important."

"I'll rest soon enough. Let me finish—and this *is* important!"

He poured her some water from the plastic pitcher, into a paper cup, and placed a straw into it. He held it for her to sip from before she started back up again.

"It came out later that the town butcher, Baker, owner of plenty white hoods, confessed he had been drinking that day.

He walked away with a temporary limp and a few scratches, while Madison's family planned her funeral."

"Look, I don't need a reminder about what happened. I didn't kill anyone. Besides, I'm going to Alcoholics Anonymous meetings now."

"I'm not telling you this to make you feel guilty, son."

"Sorry, Mama Rose, I get a little defensive when reminded. So, what happened to Baker?"

"He went to trial several months later, and old Judge Merriweather, his best friend and part of the good ol' boys' club, slapped him with just 90 days of community service."

"So, he got away with murder?"

"Pretty much. Coop withdrew for a long time. There was something different about my brother after that. He wasn't a loving person anymore. I didn't understand right then."

Michael folded his hands behind his neck.

"Maybe he just needed some time. He just lost the love of his life."

"No, he craved a darkness... Demona Stone."

"Who?"

"Demona. She was a Boo-Hag."

"A Boo-what?"

Michael massaged his perfect goatee with a fifth grader's puzzled look on his face.

"A Boo-Hag is an evil witch and shape-shifter. The elders told stories every Saturday night around the bar halls about her. I fetched them longnecks, taking a sip or two, while soaking up their tales."

"All this sounds far-fetched."

He looked into Mama Rose's lazy eyes, then watched her lilac lips move in slow motion.

"Listen, if anyone saw her reflection, that person would be left with a permanent mark to serve as a reminder of the evil vision witnessed." "You look so tired. Why don't you take a nap and finish telling me later?"

"I need to finish now, Michael!"

He took a deep breath while standing up beside her and holding her cold hands.

"Go ahead."

"When I was 13 and attended the Wraw Fair, my best friend double-dared me to look at Demona in a mirror. I lifted up his shiny pocketknife and pointed it towards where Demona had a palm-reading booth. Once I saw her image in it, I felt my hand burning from the end of the wooden handle. I dropped it to the ground, almost stabbing my right foot."

Mama Rose's hands trembled in Michael's.

"You okay? Do I need to get the nurse?"

"No, it always gets to me when I talk about her."

"Maybe this is a sign for you to stop talking about her and rest like you should've been doing."

"Nonsense. Let me finish, son. My body shook all over until I collapsed. My eyes rolled back. After a few shakes and some water splashed onto my face, I woke up."

"Honestly, this is too much for me to take in, Mama Rose," he said, as he sat back down.

"It's all true."

"Okay, whatever you say."

Michael cupped his chin in one hand, resting his elbow on his lap. "I saw Demona for the last time in Baker's store a few months later.

I was standing in the checkout line, holding a paper sack of red-hot suckers. She wrapped her long hand around my neck. Demona dug her grey hypodermic-needle-like nails, with red tips, deep into my throat. Drops of blood splashed onto my white Keds."

"Did she hurt you?"

"Yes, but what she whispered in my ear was worse than her death grip around my neck."

Mama Rose paused for several seconds, staring down at her tired and shriveled hands.

"What... what did she say?"

"I thought you weren't interested in my story, Michael."

"I'm not."

He shrugged his shoulders and glanced away from her, before quickly looking into her eyes, secretly craving more of her tale. "Well..."

"Come on, Mama Rose, tell me. I want to know."

"Okay. Demona whispered, 'You caught me off guard once, but never again. That was your free and only pass. Watch yourself, little girl! Keep your doors and windows locked, too. Tell Coop that I'll be waiting for him.' "

Michael stared into Mama Rose's eyes.

"I never told anyone, and my once-auburn hair turned snow-white that same day. My mama dyed it several times, but the color never held. That's how it remained, even to this day."

Mama Rose pulled her wig off, and white curls sprang straight up.

Michael stood to get a closer look, then ran his fingers through her hair.

"This doesn't really prove all that happened."

"You're right."

She nodded her head slowly and began to cough again, louder. She attempted to pick up her cup, but she spilled it all over herself.

"I told you that you needed your rest."

Michael called the nurse in to change her. He stepped out into the hall, until the nurse finished, then reentered.

"It just slipped out of my hands."

"Please rest."

"Don't you want to know what happened to Coop, Michael?" "No. I'm more worried about you."

"Son, no sense worrying about me. I know where I'm going. I'm worried about you. That's why I need you to hear all of this."

"Don't worry about me."

"I do."

"I'm going to call Sis to sit with you, while I go and clean up." "No. Please stay. I just have a little more to tell you. Please."

He walked back over to her bedside and sat down.

"So, how does Coop fit in with this Demona chick?" he asked, looking up at the ceiling.

"I begged him not to even think about trying to find her, but he ended up doing it, anyhow. He wanted Baker to pay. So, Demona cast a twisted spell for him. A week later, Baker went missing."

Mama Rose closed her eyes.

"You okay?"

She touched his hand, opened her heavy lids, and nodded. Her breathing began to slow down. She continued with more pauses between each word.

"Baker's wife and son found his bloody mangled body hanging in the middle of his store, as large vultures fed on it. I heard his wife lost her mind, and the son threw himself into a tree shredder on their farm."

"That's awful. I bet Coop left town after that."

"Nope. He jumped off the sharp lake cliff near FM 6969 six months later, on Halloween night, landing headfirst. Folks around here say Coop's restless spirit haunts that spot to this day, causing fatal accidents to careless drivers on that road, where Madison died."

"I didn't know that about Coop," he said, as he covered his mouth and stood up to stare out the window.

"Some claimed to have seen his old red Ford with a shiny bent-up grill and two tall black horns on the sides of the truck near the windows, with glowing, flaming tips. I saw it once and only then. I've steered as far as possible from FM 6969. So should you. Avoid it at all costs!"

Michael turned around to face her and leaned against the window with his arms crossed.

"Okay, I'm gonna call Sis."

He walked back to her and kissed her bony hand, and then he headed towards the door.

"Here, take this crucifix, my boy, and wear it always. I prayed a very powerful prayer over it."

He turned around and went to her bedside.

"You know I don't believe in stuff like this. I never have."

"Please, Michael, take it. Promise me that you will keep it close to you at all times." "Give it here."

He rolled his eyes and frowned, as she dropped it into his baby-soft hands. He buried it in the back pocket of his *Gucci* jeans.

He bent over to hug her, and then she was gone.

Michael stayed until a caretaker from Wraw & Son's Funeral Home arrived to transport her. He attended the memorial service and stayed a few extra days to help Wichita out with Mama Rose's estate.

On Halloween night, he packed, loaded his vehicle, and backed out of her driveway. Wichita waved him on, as she pulled her heavy multi- colored shawl tighter around her shoulders.

Michael waved back to her, as he turned to a jazz channel on his satellite radio while positioning JD closer to him. He stared at the crucifix; it rested in the passenger's seat. He threw it into his immaculate glove compartment without a second thought.

After driving a few miles from Mama Rose's house, which was then his sister's, and passing the hospital, he noticed a work convoy with flashing signs: Entry Ramp Closed for Construction.

Alternate routes were entered into his GPS—Cedar Lane or FM 6969.

He looked up through his sunroof and whispered, "Mama Rose, wherever you are, I love you."

He made a left turn onto FM 6969.

Within seconds, he heard loud noises coming up fast behind him. His heart raced like a rabbit being chased by a pack of wolves. His eyes twitched, and his hands trembled on the steering wheel. In his rearview mirror, he saw only young kids packed in a neon yellow convertible.

Michael sighed and lifted up JD. He screwed the cap off and pressed his lips to its glass mouth and tilted it back, as he kept his eyes on the road. He then secured the bottle between his legs.

Just then, an old truck with flaming horn tips appeared ahead of the convertible. The driver of the car blew the horn constantly and flashed his high beams. The car passed the truck with loud laughter filling the chilly night air, accompanied by *Pour Some Sugar on Me,* blaring from the speakers.

The kids threw bottles at the truck, which picked up unbelievable speed. The flaming horns lowered and rammed the convertible on both of its sides and raised it off the road, tossing it up almost a hundred feet in the air. The horns retracted back into their original position, as the convertible exploded before it hit the asphalt.

Michael pulled over onto the side of the road to catch his breath while resting his sweaty palms and head on the steering wheel.

He tore his glove compartment door off its hinges to find the crucifix. Once he got his hands around it, he held onto it tight as if it was going to fly away. His pants were soaked with more than just the JD spill.

Before Michael could grab something from the back to dry himself off, he heard a loud etching sound from his windshield.

He looked up and read the bloody, sooty message:

You're real lucky. Consider this your last pass.

The End.

Case File: #88783

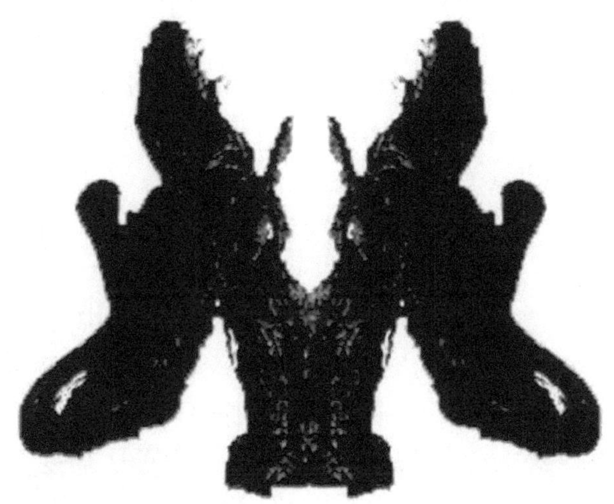

Leviticus by David. W. Landrum

My friends told me it happens. Most everyone gets dumped at one time or another; just notice how many songs there are about it, they said.

That's true, I guess, but when it happens to you, it goes from being something people write songs about to being a wound and a pain that blights your whole life. When I told this to Eloise Lawry, the girl who took him away from me, she said, "Marcie, I don't care. I'm not even sorry. He's mine now. You lost, I won. Live with it." That got my blood boiling so much I decided I would take revenge on her—get even somehow. I wanted it to hurt her. I wanted to cause her pain but wasn't sure how I could do it.

I would not do anything stupid. Shooting her, hiring a hit man, setting her house on fire were not options. Like I said, these things have consequences. Frustration led to the remark I made to my sister about how I'd like to do something really nasty but it would take an evil spell to do it. She replied, jokingly, "Maybe you ought to talk to Leviticus."

Leviticus was a girl—a woman now—I had been friends with in high school She practiced witchcraft. Lots of women I've known say they practice magic, but she really did. She was a sorceress. Back in high school everyone was afraid of her. My girlfriends said she was creepy. A lot of guys thought she was wacked out. The born-again kids were always trying to convert her. I thought she was cool and admired her good looks.

Leviticus was pretty, tall, athletic. She and I ran track together, though her senior year she quit the team to devote herself to the magical arts. She had red hair and blue eyes. She always wore black, whether she put on a long dress or a mini (she never wore pants, always dresses). She did the Goth thing: heavy eye make-up, black lipstick and nails, weird-looking jewelry. The kids in school excluded her and did so with the usual tactics of rumor, insult, and shunning. Outwardly, she shook it off, but I knew she was lonely and so I hung around with her. We ate together and saw each other between classes and when school ended and in the morning. I even hung with her when Daryl Jodry crossed her with such dire results and so many people backed off, too scared to try to bully her.

Daryl played football. He started a rumor that Leviticus had gone down for the whole team and spread it all through the school. People sort of didn't believe it, but you know how it is in high school: rumors become quasi-facts even if people don't believe them entirely. Pretty soon everyone at school believed she really had let all the guys on the team screw her.

"She did it for money," one of my track teammates said, "so she could buy the things she needs to do the witchcraft stuff."

The talk grew and grew, so much that Leviticus confronted Jodry one day in the cafeteria, in front of practically the whole school.

"Stop telling lies about me," she warned him.

He smirked up at her from his seat.

"Is the truth hurting you too much?" he smirked.

"I'm warning you," she returned. "Don't push this anymore or you'll pay the price."

He laughed. People sneered, though they were uneasy. Leviticus (her real name was Carol-Lynn Parsons) looked scary that day. She had on a black, draped blouse, a short black skirt, black tights, and boots. She had braded her hair on one side and wound some kind of red metallic fiber through it. It looked like blood. And she did not evince the least bit of fear at Jodry — only contempt. She looked at him as if he was an annoying insect she did not want to swat but now had no choice but to do so.

Jodry died the next day.

He died during a football game. Someone tackled him. When he and he guy from the other team got up, Jodry smiled but then stiffened, and went pale (I was at the game, had a good seat and saw it all close up). Blood burst from his nose and eyes and he crumpled to the ground. He lay there convulsing and foaming at the mouth as his teammates and the school sports doctor tried to revive him. He never got up. Coroners said heart failure was the cause of death. Everyone at school remembered Leviticus' threat to him.

She got some flak for this. Jodry's parents threatened to sue her because they claimed her threat had created psychological tension that led to his heart failure. Of course, they didn't have a leg to stand on, legally. And Leviticus said she had not threatened him, only warned him that the kind of behavior he had engaged in brought about bad consequences.

Everyone was afraid of her after that—even the teachers. I stayed friends with her. One day in the cafeteria (we were at a table by ourselves); she asked me if I ever thought of doing magic.

"Not really."

"Would you like to learn?"

I pondered. "I don't know. It seems like something you have to give your whole life to."

"It is, but it's got big payoffs. I'll teach you if you want to learn—if you ever decide you want to, let me know."

I never did get back with her about the magic. After graduation, we went to different colleges and lost contact with each other. When my sister mentioned her, though, I decided to find her.

It wasn't hard. She had a Facebook page. I friended her and sent her a message that I wanted to get together.

We met at a coffee bar. She came in looking very un-Leviticus. She wore a blue skirt and white blouse, sandals and a bucket hat. She smiled and, to my surprise, bent down and gave me a kiss on the cheek.

"Wow," I said. "I hardly recognize you because you're not wearing black."

"I got tired of wearing the same thing every day. There are too many nice colors to wear black all the time. It was a high school thing—plus I was trying to establish my identity."

We talked. Leviticus owned a fashion shop in one of the malls in town. I had shopped there a few times. It was a popular, successful business.

"How did you get the idea to start a business?"

"I majored in business at Michigan State. I had a little money, so I used it as start-up funds. Luckily, the place took off."

"Do you still do magic?"

She regarded me a moment.

"Sure I do."

"I need your help."

She asked how I needed her help. I told her about how Cameron had dumped me for Eloise and how it was all her doing. I vented quite a bit. It felt good to let off a little steam. Leviticus did not give me the tired old platitudes everyone else threw at me when I told my story. She didn't tell me how break-ups happen, how everyone goes through them, how I needed to forget and move on. She just listened. When I had finished, she settled back in her chair.

"So what do you want?"

I leaned in close to her. "I want you to make her pay—like you made Daryl Jodry pay for what he did to you."

"You want her dead?"

"I do."

"Isn't that a little much, Marcie?"

"Not for what she did to me. And don't tell me it happens all the time, Carol-Lynn. She had no right to break us up. We both know what an arrogant little slut she is. I only want her to get what she has coming for what she did to me and twenty other girls the past few years."

"Do you think what you want fits what she did?"

"Cameron will come back to me, but only if she is gone. I'm willing to pay you."

"When I do magic for people, it's my custom to let them pay what they think they should pay me."

"I don't have a lot of money. I can give you a thousand." "I'll take it."

"And you'll kill her?"

"It doesn't work like that. Human life is not mine to give or take." "It isn't? You killed Daryl."

"I didn't kill him. I simply opened the door to justice. Through his desire to hurt, he had weakened his resistance to the forces of evil who always want to destroy us but are held back by certain forces from doing so. He was vulnerable. When I do that kind of magic, I only weaken the protection people like him have. The results can vary."

I felt nervous when she said this.

"Okay, you can't kill anyone, I get that. Couldn't you weaken the protection Eloise has around her? She seems a lot like Jodry."

"It's different with her. I'm not allowed to talk about it."

"How about something else? Could you send a monster against her? You wouldn't be responsible if the monster killed her."

"I'm afraid I can't do that. It's too dangerous." Leviticus paused then added, "This seems like a really big deal to you, Marcie."

"It is."

"Well, if Cameron left you, maybe he isn't the kind of guy you want to be a relationship with. And haven't you ever broken up with a guy? I remember Norman."

Norman Reed was a guy I had dated in high school. I dumped him. He took it pretty hard.

"That," I said, "is beside the point. And you're starting to sound like everybody else. How about you? Have you ever been stabbed in the back by someone who is a born manipulator?"

"Several times."

"You didn't retaliate?"

"No."

"Why not?"

"I always wondered if my evaluation of their actions was correct." I got up.

"Never mind. I guess I'll have to do this myself."

I stomped out and left her there. I didn't know what I was going to do, but a trip to the library seemed like a good idea. I walked four long blocks, went in, and sat down at a table in the stacks. Leviticus was there, right beside me. She appeared just a second after I sat down, though I didn't see her "materialize" or anything like that. She was just there. My astonishment overcame my anger.

"You followed me?"

"Sort of."

I felt a twinge of remorse for having taken off when she had been gracious enough to meet with me. I apologized.

"It's all right. I know you're planning to find a book of spells and will start trying to do this on your own. Not a good idea—kind of like trying to teach yourself to use a nuclear reactor. I'll help you. I could send a monster. Do you still want me to do that?"

"Yes."

"Okay. What you're asking is dangerous. If you're dead set on it, though, we'll work something out. It's dangerous to try to do magic when you don't know what you're doing. I don't want to see you hurt."

"I'm flattered," I said, my voice sarcastic, my anger returning.

"In high school you were one of the few people who treated me like I wasn't a freak in a circus sideshow. That meant a lot of me. I'm afraid I didn't show you how much it meant. I could have been a better friend, but I was too caught up in learning the craft to pay much attention to anything but that, which is something I very much regret. If you want to target Eloise, I'll tell you how."

"I want to, Leviticus. I won't be able to rest till I do." "I'll show you what you need to do."

"So can I send a monster to get her? A werewolf or a zombie?"

"A rakshasa would be better."

"What's that?"

"A demon from India. They're nasty. They live off human flesh. They're vicious, evil, poisonous, and hard to control. If you want it to attack Eloise, though, you'll have summon it yourself."

The thought of having to deal with a supernatural creature Leviticus had called "dangerous" scared me.

"Why do I have to summon it myself?"

"Despite what you think, I can't kill anyone. I didn't kill Jodry. I can't kill Eloise for you. You'll have to call the thing to come and serve you. They are violent, vicious creatures. The only way you can command it is by drawing a magic circle and standing inside it. I'll set the template so that it contains the summons. You won't have to say anything. Once you close the circle, the creature will appear. A rakshasa can read your mind. Once it looks into your thoughts, it will know what to do."

"How do I draw the circle?"

Leviticus took out a sheet of paper and a blue gel pen. "I'll draw it for you. Copy it exactly as I set it down. The reason you draw it is for protection. The rakshasa can't cross the double line if it is correctly drawn. Make it exactly like this. Stand in the circle until the rakshasa returns to seek release or it will be all over for you."

"What will it do to me?"

Leviticus met my eyes. "It will eat you alive." I nodded, folded the paper and thanked her.

"Thank me when you're past all of this. I've got to go." "I'll get the money for you."

She shook her head. "I'll do this gratis."

She gave a few instructions and went over the sketch with me, pointing out some important features in the diagram. When she was finished I nodded and put the paper in my purse. When I looked up, Leviticus was gone.

I went home afraid and reflective. Still, I had my resolution. The urge to kill Eloise bubbled up like black volcanic mud from deep inside me and it lit the fire for revenge. Getting herself eaten alive was just what she deserved. After the sun set, after three stars became visible in the sky, I began the spell.

I drew the circle in white chalk on the slate floor by the front entrance to my house. I copied the pattern Leviticus had given me very carefully.

After a moment, the temperature in my living room dropped. I shivered even though I had on pants and a sweatshirt. Things started to look crazy — that's the only way I can describe it. The familiar things in my front room — furniture, knick-knacks, paintings on the walls, even curtains and carpets — looked sinister, like in a nightmare. I thought they might come to life and jump at me. Then I smelled an odd odor — a combination of spices like turmeric and cumin but also of rotten meat and the way I smell when a guy has really turned me on and I'm wet and dripping. Right in front of my eyes, a creature took shape.

At first its form looked faint — a dark blue smudge of light. It quickly became distinct. I saw the outline its body, arms, shoulders, trunk, legs, head. Its features appeared. Cold terror fell on me like a shower of icy water. The thing was female. I saw breasts and a cunt. As I said, it was dark blue. It had red eyes, fangs, a darting forked tongue, claws and hair that writhed like snakes — like Medusa's hair. The ugliness of it paralyzed me. It focused it red eyes on me transformed so it turned flat, like a snake, slid under my door, and was gone.

I relaxed. The things in the room returned to normal. It scared me to remember that I had been sitting next to, and mouthing off to, the woman who could control such gruesome, loathsome creatures as the one I had just seen. I wondered how long it would take the monster to accomplish her mission.

I had to wait in the circle. Leviticus did not explain it, but I deduced that the creature might come back at any time. If it caught me out of the circle's protection, I would not be able to get back to safety in time. I imagined the monster could move more swiftly than a human being.

However swiftly it could move, I ended up standing for two hours in the circle. Inevitably nature took its course—the wrong course for this situation. I had to go. I had been so caught up with the preparations for summoning the rakshasa, I had forgotten to make a pre-emptive a trip to the bathroom.

But I didn't dare step outside the circle. It would be like an old episode of The Twilight Zone—like the guy who survives a nuclear war, realizes he will finally have all kinds of time to read, and then breaks his glasses. A girl is killed by a monster because she makes a trip to the pisser.

But it was getting unbearable. Then I saw the solution an arm's length away. I laughed. The old thunder mug, as we called it when we were kids.

We used them a lot at the drive-in movie. We would go there and have to take a whiz, but we didn't want to miss any of the movies; and, anyway, the rest rooms at the drive-in were dirty and smelly. So we would keep our drink cups and, if we really had to go, would pee in them and dump it out the door of the car. My brothers and I would respect each other's privacy and decency—no peeking. It worked as a system and became a big joke with us. I reached over to a shelf and easily plucked a decorative container —actually, a glass jar full of marbles.

I poured the marbles out on the floor. They rolled to one side, resting in a low spot where the slate joined the staircase. I knew, from years of living here, how that part of the floor was uneven, which was good because the marbles would bunch up there and not roll all over the place.

In the privacy of my own home, I pulled down my pants and underwear, squatted, and did my business. I was careful no urine got out to erase part of the circle. When I finished, I put the jar of urine on one of the steps (it looked gross) and waited, quite pleased with myself.

Fifteen minutes later, I felt the monster I had summoned approach, like a tidal wave of evil and of smells. The thing came through an open window this time.

According to what Leviticus had told me, the creature would return, its assignment finished, see if it could kill me, notice I was in the magic circle, bow, and return to wherever it came from.

The thing approached. I noticed its hands and mouth were covered with blood. Eloise's blood, I surmised. As I watched it, an evil leer spread over its black lips. It bared its sharp teeth. Its red eyes flickered. I thought it would leave and go on its way, but, with snake-liked speed it moved toward me, across the chalk line of the magic circle, and seized me by the throat.

I screamed. The creature made a sound like a pig squealing, but lower. I heard a note of triumph in its voice. Its arms gripped me from behind and then transformed to tentacles, wrapping around my neck and stomach, slimy, cold, burning my flesh like acid as the thing pulled me toward it. I felt its breasts against my back and its nauseating hot breath on my neck. I screamed, but the rakshasa began to choke me with its tentacle so no sound came out of my mouth.

The tentacle around my neck and waist held me firm. My body burned as if someone had poured acid on my skin. A hand (how many limbs did it have?) seized my right arm and pulled it straight up.

I wondered why, and in a moment I knew. The rakshasa put two of my fingers in its mouth and bit down on them. It did not snap them off but slowly bit through them, crushing them in a slow-chapped motion. I screamed more loudly. I started to lose consciousness. It was poisoning me. My head began to spin. Numbness and lethargy took me over.

As my vision faded, I saw the marbles on the floor and realized how the demonic thing killing me—eating me alive—had got into the circle. The marbles. They lay in a dark red column, blotting out a portion of the circle. I kicked at them. They scattered, rolling away, uncovering the lines and the inscriptions.

The rakshasa howled in pain. It let go of my neck so I could breathe again. I felt the burning, numbing tentacle slide off my stomach as well. Sizzling sounds, the sound of howling, the smell, now, of the thing's burning flesh, assaulted my senses. I sank to my knees. I knew I had to stay upright. If I fell, I would tumble outside the circle and the creature would finish me off.

I looked up. It stood by the side of the circle and knelt on one knee. Its skin smoked. Black blood poured from gashes on its breasts and stomach. Then, to my dulled surprise, it made namskar, putting its hands together and bowing its head. That done, it faded from my vision.

I could sense it was gone. The aura of evil it carried with it dissipated.

The stench of it, along with its spicy, sexy smell, completely faded.

I collapsed on the floor with a heavy thump, remembering what Leviticus had said about the rakshasa being poisonous. I felt cold spread through my body. I felt what Eloise must have felt. Did I deserve it? Was I being punished for taking revenge? Nausea spread over me. My head started to spin. I looked up, focusing on the jar of urine on the stairs. I laughed. It seemed supreme irony that a jar of yellow piss would be the last thing I saw before I died.

***

Of course, I did not die. I would not be able to tell you this story if I had. I woke up in a hospital bed. My eyes focused on the monitoring equipment. I raised my head and heard someone get up. In a moment, Leviticus came to my bedside and touched me gently.

"Quiet. Lie still."

I nodded. My head hurt and my right hand felt like it had been plunged in scalding water.

"What happened?" she asked me.

"I dropped something that blotted out the circle. I was able to kick it away at the last minute."

I lifted my hand. The doctors had swathed my fingers in thick bandages with metal supporting splints.

"They were able to reattach your fingers. I know it hurts, but be thankful you even lived through the attack."

"Eloise?"

"It will be on the news tonight. Better you see it for yourself."

"The rakshasa poisoned me," I said. "How did I survive?"

"I knew right away you were hurt. I went to your place and gave you a potent to counteract the poison. Then I called the EMTs. They got you to the ER. I told them I had seen a dog running out of your house. I didn't want your injuries to look too similar to Eloise's. I erased the magic circle." She smiled. "I even got rid of the jar of urine you left on the steps."

"What did the rakshasa do to Eloise? Did it eat her?"

"No. It bit her and watched her die. Dying from the kind of poison they inject into a person is not a quick or a pleasant way to go. As she died, it tore at her. In other words, it tortured her to death. That's why it took so long for the rakshasa to return to you—two hours of agony and of being taunted, slashed and bitten, menaced, and abused by an ugly monster. That's how she made her exit."

"Good. I got a little taste of what the poison was like." "I'm sorry you got hurt."

"I lived. She died. That's all that matters."

"When your fingers are better—well, I do have some healing powers. I'll see if I we can get them completely well. And there's something else."

My mouth felt dry. "What?"

"I told you how magic works, Marcie. Jodry died because he lived in a way that made him vulnerable to evil. I opened the door, and evil took him. Has this brush with the supernatural enlightened you in any way?"

I paused and then said, "Cameron."

She nodded solemnly. "Yes. You see it. That tells me you are a good candidate to learn magic. I felt that when we were in high school but didn't follow it up. Now is the time for you to start learning."

"If I learn magic the first thing I want to do is go after him. The more I think about him, the more I see that Eloise was only half of the equation. Cameron is the other half—and the worst half. It was more him than her. I want to kill him. I want him to suffer more than she did. I see now how stupid I was to go after Eloise and not see that he is the cause of it all and deserves the worst of it."

She smiled and raised her eyebrows. "I see now that you're a real candidate. You feel something strongly enough to want to give your soul for it."

"I'll give my soul just to hurt him."

"You don't need to do that—not for the kind of magic I practice. But I think we can work something out."

For just a moment my mind filled with all the old horror scripts I remembered—more Twilight Zone stuff: the woman gets her revenge, but in the end she is enslaved or ends up worse off than before because a witch or sorcerer or the Devil put a clause in the contract or the agreement. Leviticus might double-cross me to take advantage of me. But then the dark fire, the thirst for vengeance, the lust to hurt, to avenge the wrong Cameron had done to me a hundred times, welled up like a pitch-black tide breaking in a wave inside me.

Leviticus looked into my eyes. She saw what I felt.

"I was afraid you would start fooling around with magic and spells and destroy yourself. That's why I didn't want to help you at first. Now I see some good came out of it. The whole episode set your sights strait. Now you see clearly what Cameron did to you—and what you might be able to do to him. I'll teach you. I'll also protect you."

"Protect me from what?"

"Eloise had some friends you might be surprised to know about. I know about them because it's my business—and I don't mean by fashion store business. They might come after you. I knew that but didn't think you would listen if I warned you. You wanted revenge too badly."

"And now I'm in danger?"

"No. I can protect you. I will. And you can protect yourself."
"How?"

"Do what I say. The first charms you learn will be ones of self-protection. After that, you can destroy the petty little amateurs who will try to attack you. Then we can think up something very special—and very unpleasant—for Cameron."

We heard the nurse coming.

"I'll be back. As soon as they release you from the hospital, you can begin your training."

Leviticus disappeared.

A nurse came in and checked my monitors. A doctor arrived and asked me what had happened. I told him something came into the house and attacked me. Some kind of animal, I said, probably a dog. He filled out a report. He said he wanted to keep me here until they could test for rabies. He left. They transferred me to a regular hospital room. A nurse examined my fingers and said she couldn't believe how quickly they were healing. She gave me an injection for the pain. I called my parents and my brother and told them what had happened. They said they would be there right away.

By now it was 6:00 and time for the local news. The pain medication made me groggy, but I fought to stay awake. FOX 17 News came on. A pretty blonde anchorwoman began the program with a grave look on her face.

"Police are investigating the enigmatic death young women on the north side of Grand Rapids," she said. "Eloise Lawry was found dead in her apartment at four a.m. this morning, apparently of a snake bite. But forensic scientists say the venom they found in her system was like none they have ever encountered in all their years of dealing with snakebite victims." The scene switched to a group of puzzled forensic scientists and a toxicologist. None of them had seen anything like this, they said, and knew of no venomous snake or insect that produced this sort of poison."

I listened with satisfaction. I had paid a price for this. My fingers were maimed and, now, I had to give my life to Leviticus and to learning magic. But I didn't care. When I gave Cameron his justice, there would be no repercussions. I lay in the hospital bed and smiled as the pain medication slowly carried me away to sleep.

The End.

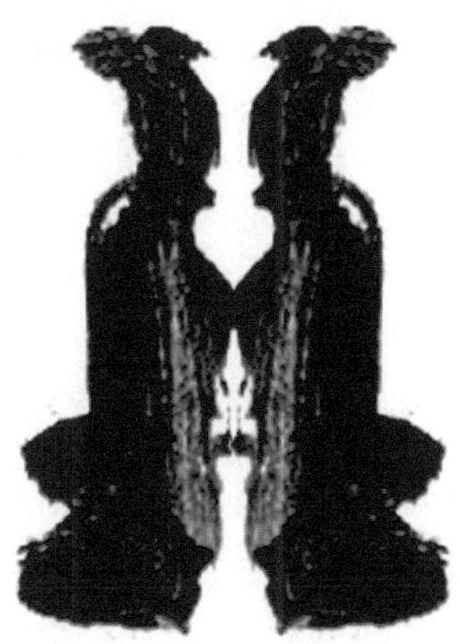

Bringing In the Sheaves by Richard Thomas

Ever since I was a little boy, the cornfields filled my nightmares with the sounds of rustling stalks, and the stench of something decomposing. I guess you could call it a recurring dream, the way the empty fields would fill my head with gentle hot winds and stinging scratches up and down my arms. I blame it on my younger brother, Billy—it was his idea after all, his fault. But I don't hold onto that grudge. I see the girl, Margie, every once in awhile, hanging out in front of the 7-11 or maybe down by the bowling alley. Small town living doesn't offer up many options, but back then she was one of them—today, less so.

Doesn't really matter the name of our town, they're all the same, dotted across the Midwest, filling up the middle of Illinois, long arteries of dust and despair stretching out in every direction. Bluford, Cairo, Dakota—we all worked the fields, tending to chickens, hogs, cows and the like. It was a lot of early morning chores and dark nights where we tried to kill ourselves one way or another.

My younger brother Billy, only three years my junior, he'd tag along whenever he could. Sometimes I needed somebody to shoot hoops with on the back of the barn, or to blame the broken window on, that's how it went. He was always falling down, his simple skull filled with ideas, massive forehead constantly scratched and riddled with scabs. I didn't treat him like a simpleton, but he was definitely slow. I'd hear a thud or a slam, something creaking or snapping in two, and I'd go running for the barn, running for the tractor that kept moving into the cornfield, with nobody on top of it, as it disappeared into the unforgiving folds. A tine of a pitchfork jammed through his meaty thigh, trying to fly out of the loft into a pile of hay below. An angry raccoon disappearing down the dirt road, unwilling to be his pet, Billy's face and arms bleeding, his wide grin stretched taut over bones that knew no failure. One dead animal or another, cradled in his arms—a hen with a snapped neck, or field mice staged around a tiny table sipping at tea, a stiff cat swung around by its tail. He didn't mean anything by it, just curious, I guess. We all are.

The girl lived down the road a bit. She was always dirty, constantly lifting her torn skirt over her head, showing off her dingy underwear to whoever would look. But she was sweet on me, sweet on Billy. Margie was a year ahead of me. She probably just wanted somewhere quiet to go where her daddy couldn't touch her, where her mother couldn't lay her dead eyes on Margie's thin arms and pale skin. So we let her come over, after school, or in the summertime. We'd pal around with her down by the creek, looking for tadpoles, or frogs to put in jars, left out on a shelf where they'd dry up and leave our room stinking of something gone foul—rotten and thick.

When she asked us to tie her up, we thought she was joking. We were older now, sixth grade for me, about twelve, and Billy only nine. I had seen a filmstrip in class once, bad illustrations of flaccid penises, the scientific data going over my head, our stunned faces flush and embarrassed by the idea of a naked woman's body, the idea of what we were supposed to do. It was dirty. And yet, it was spectacular.

We'd seen her underwear before, it wasn't a big deal, and we weren't interested in putting our tongues in her mouth. Gross. But we had nothing else to do, so we tied Margie to a post at the back of the barn, and turned to each other, mute, as she smiled in the dimly lit space. We ignored her for a bit, leaving her to squirm, to test the knots, moaning and grunting. She was our kidnapped ransom, so we went about the barn fortifying our defense, leaning broken broom handles against the wall, our weapons, gathering shovels and baseball bats, and a lone, rusty pitchfork, still stained with a bit of Billy's blood.

Billy finally approached her and licked her face, from her chin to her eyebrow, and she giggled and turned her head away. He spit into the dirt.

"Salty," he said.

He picked up a stick and started poking her, in the belly at first, and then he raised and lowered her faded skirt.

"Billy?" I asked.

He glanced at me, then back to Margie, a dirty grin easing across his face.

"What? She started this."

Margie turned to look at me, her eyes tiny fragments of coal.

"Leave him alone, Rodney," she said, "We're just playing."

"Yeah, Rodney," my brother wheezed, bending over, and raising her skirt. "Let's see what she's got."

I crossed my arms. I wanted to see too. I glanced to the house, and it was quiet, nobody in sight. Billy held her skirt up with the stick, as Margie smiled, and took his other hand and placed it between her legs.

"Nothin," Billy said. "She ain't got nothin."

A car skidded into the yard and Billy let her skirt fall back down, and quickly untied her from the post. His face was splotchy and red, as was hers, but I was cold and pale, on the verge of throwing up.

"I better get home," Margie said. "Almost dinner."

She leaned over and kissed me on the cheek, and skipped out of the barn, into the sunlight. I wiped my face, the sticky residue of strawberry bubblegum, Billy's eyes on me, glassy and empty.

***

It was all Billy could talk about—Margie. All summer long. I didn't see her again, not for a while, but he went looking for her whenever he could. He looked for her at the grocery store with mother, whenever we went for a ride with dad, fishing or off on some errand. He leaned out of the beat up Chevy Nova like a dog, his tongue flapping in the wind.

My father always plowed a section of the back forty, a path out into the corn, with a patch of it cleared out, like his private sitting room. There wasn't much in the space, just a rusty metal chair and a crate filled with empty beer bottles, a hole dug into the earth filled with cigarette butts and spent matches. I don't blame my father for wanting this space, somewhere away from our mother, who had an endless list of things for him to do— broken latches and busted screens to fix, buckets of paint that needed to be emptied. As far as I know, he'd just sit out there in the dark, staring up at the stars, drinking and smoking, wishing to be someplace else. Anywhere else.

On the rare evenings when the two of them would go upstairs, turning the television set up loud, hand in hand as they climbed the stairs, all giggles and fists of flesh, Billy and I would head for the fields, to sit in his chair, and stare at the sky. It was as close as we'd get to the man, as close as he'd let us get. We'd find half smoked butts and smoke them, coughing and spitting onto the ground. We'd drink the warm remnants from the bottom of the bottles and cans, sweet and sour and forbidden.

When Billy started disappearing, this was the place I went. I often found him covered in blood. He wouldn't say anything, just hold his palms up to me and grin. I'd take him back to the house and clean him up, hosing him down until he started to cry, and then I'd slap him until he shut up.

Margie started showing up again, and she and Billy would disappear into the barn. They had secrets now, would go quiet when I walked into the barn. We'd still take walks together, to the creek and into the woods, even out into the cornfields, lost and scratched by the sharp stalks and ears, hollering for each other, hiding, as we choked on the dust and the heat. Inevitably we'd end up in my father's room, lying by the chair, the walls of corn around us a fortress against the rest of the world. I only saw them kiss once, but it made my stomach curl. He was too young, I thought, and even though he was my brother, he was clueless about Margie's advances. I barely understood them myself.

I cornered Margie one afternoon and warned her off my brother. She put one hand on her hip and asked me if I wanted that attention, if her time spent with my brother was something that I'd prefer she reserve for me? I told her she was crazy, but she wasn't wrong. And on an afternoon when Billy wasn't around, she and I ended up in the hayloft, our wet mouths on each other, my stomach in knots, telling myself this was what I needed to do in order to protect my brother, my hands on her dirty, sweaty body, our tongues a slick disaster.

***

Daddy had been on the road now for weeks. Business trip, local fair, something to do with the price of our harvest and subsidies, I didn't understand it all. I knew that the house was quiet—that we were bored to death, and I knew that the bottle of whiskey that hid above the fridge was slowly emptying as our mother sat quiet at the kitchen table.

We siphoned off part of it, and replaced it with water, disappearing into the fields when she went to sleep. We choked it down as we lay in the darkness, waiting for something to happen. When I drifted off, his hands found my neck, his knees on my shoulders—the air in my lungs

disappearing into the night. He'd found out about us, Margie and me, there was nothing else to explain it. He was stronger then I remembered, his eyes bulging in his head as his squeezed on my neck, showing no sign of letting up. I finally brought my knees up, banging him in the center of his back, throwing him off of me, as air rushed back into my lungs.

"Damnit, Billy," I choked. "She's not worth it. You're too young, anyway."

"Fuck you," he murmured, looking up from the ground, the darkness swallowing our sweat and our tension.

"She's my girl," Billy muttered. "Don't touch her again."

"You'd choose flesh over blood?" I asked. "She's just some stupid whore from down the road."

"Shut your mouth, Rodney."

"I'm sure I'm not the only boy she's kissing. I told you, she's no good." Billy lay there.

"That's for me to decide," he said.

***

Daddy never did come back from that business trip. And that wasn't a good thing. Billy wasn't talking to me — a ghost that drifted about the property, chucking rocks at anything that moved. For three days we didn't talk, until I walked past the barn and the stench of rotten meat engulfed me.

I'd let him have the barn, somewhere to go where he didn't have to look at my face. In the middle of the sweltering barn lay a large metal bowl of cat food, dusted with white powder, and surrounding it was a ring of dead cats. Flies buzzed my face, their grey tongues protruding from their tiny still mouths.

Billy.

I yelled for him, but he didn't answer. I headed for the cornfields as sweat pushed out of every pore.

I found him standing over Margie, her arms tied behind her, sitting in the metal chair, buck naked and crying. Billy was holding a pocketknife in his hand, looming over her, poking her skin with the sharp blade. Her whimpers were lost on the wind, but her eyes bore into me.

"Billy," I said. "Enough."

He turned to me, his jaw clenched.

"We're just playing," he said. Margie shook her head back and forth, afraid to speak, and Billy backhanded her across the face.

"Stop it, Billy," I said. "It's over, let her go."

"She came here," he said. "She took off her own clothes, she sat in the chair. This is what she wants," he whined.

"No, Billy, it isn't. You've gone too far."

"No, this is going too far," he said, leaning over the girl. I started running to him, but I wasn't fast enough. He put the blade under her left nipple, her breasts hardly anything at all.

81

Her eyes went wide as his thumb held the tiny pink protuberance, and he sliced it clean off and flung it to the ground. She gasped, unable to scream, as blood ran down her pale skin. He looked up at me, smiling, and I was on him, and we were rolling to the ground, my fists beating about his head, the tiny blade stabbing my back, my arms, until I knocked it out of his hand. I beat him until he stopped moving, and then I stood up.

Margie was crying, snot running down her lip, blood pooling in her lap.

"It's all right, it's over," I said.

I picked up the blade and walked to her, cutting the rope that bound her trembling flesh. I knelt down and held her as she sobbed into my shoulder. Straightening up, I held her face in my hands.

"Margie, don't come back here. You hear?" She nodded her head and quickly got dressed.

***

With daddy gone it didn't take much for mother to drift away too. She'd picked up a job at the local diner, and we saw her less and less. Strange men came for the harvest, and we watched them descend on the farm like locust. Billy and I didn't talk any more.

When the summer ended and a cool wind started to fill the space that used to be our family farm, I went to the barn in search of Billy, ready to bury the hatchet, to move on from these transgressions, to erase from our minds what had happened out there in the fields.

A shadow swung back and forth across the opening of the barn, the stiff bodies of the sacrificial cats long gone, but the rotten stench still remaining.

I swallowed a lump in my throat and stared up at the rafters, at his still body, the rope around his neck, his purple face, and a stain of urine in the dirt below his dead body. I took a breath, exhaled, and lowered my head. It didn't have to be this way.

Or maybe it did.

The End.

Case File: #21350

A Run up the Stairs by Raymond Esposito

The first night Ashley made it all the way to the twelfth step before she heard the footsteps behind her. Although "footsteps" may have been a generalization as it was certainly the sound of something coming up the stairs, but the sound definitely was not of human feet.

She was too frightened to look back into the stairwell's utter blackness and face her pursuer. Instead, she ran the remaining five stairs, turned quickly into the hall and fled into the guest room. She slammed the door harder than she had intended. The loud bang scared her because it seemed to confirm that something had indeed chased her. She tried to calm her racing heart. She found the wall switch that operated the small bedside lamp and the room brightened under the warm glow. She listened at the door but beyond it came no further proof that something waited on the other side. She laughed aloud at her own active imagination. She had often scared herself with imagined noises.

Reason returned and she rationalized that the alleged sounds were just the result of too many horror films and from being alone in a large, unfamiliar house. The month-long housesitting job was an excellent opportunity to rest while she took off a semester between her undergraduate and graduate studies. The large two-story Victorian home with its secluded countryside location had seemed the perfect place to spend October. Four glorious and relaxing weeks to read, watch movies, and explore the deep autumn woods was more of a vacation then she had ever experienced. In was perfect – in theory at least.

The Murphy's had paid her a thousand dollars in advance for sitting their New England home while they attended the birth of their first grandchild somewhere in California. They also offered her the use of the old pick-up truck that sat in the long driveway. Ashley had thanked them, but hadn't mentioned that she didn't know how to drive a stick shift. It didn't matter, the house was well stocked with food and anything else she might need she could hike the four miles into town and purchase from the small general store. On the day she arrived in the small town, the Murphy's part-time handyman had met her at the bus station and driven her to the house. He was an old skinny guy who looked about a hundred years old. He didn't speak a word on the short trip, which was fine with her. She wanted to use this little retreat to get away from people. No cell phones, no Facebook, no Internet and most of all…no drama.

When they pulled up the long drive, the old man stopped his truck and turned to her. He seemed to measure her for a moment and Ashley wondered if he expected a tip.

"You gonna be here alone?" he asked in his country accent.

She thought about lying, but then decided that the old man was harmless.

"Yep, all by my lonesome."

"Hmph," was all he said.

She opened the passenger door when he again spoke.

"Well, you jes make sure not to go down in the basement," he warned her in his heavy accent.

"Why?" she asked. She had no intention of going into the basement, but she didn't like the idea of this old guy thinking he was in charge.

"Cuz it's dark and filled with all kinds stuff a woman could get hurt on," he said.

"I'll be careful," she responded. She had no idea why she didn't just agree, but after Mike...well Mike didn't matter but she still didn't want to be bossed around anymore.

"There are a lot of brown recluse spiders in the basement," the old man added. "In Autumn they get ornery and aggressive. One bites ya, best be sure to call fer a doctor right quick."

Her expression revealed her repulsion and that seemed to satisfy the old man.

He looked at her a while longer and appeared to contemplate his next words.

"I suppose you have one of dem cellular phones," he said.

Ashley had let her contract run out two months ago and she had not renewed it.

"Nope, no cell phone."

"Well there's a house phone, my number is on a little card right next to it. Names Foster. You call me or the missus if you need anything or there's any trouble."

"Thank you, Mr. Foster I will," she said and smiled. She felt bad over having been so obstinate about the basement. The old guy was just concerned.

"No problem missy," he said.

As she stepped out of the truck, he spoke to her again.

"It's pretty safe in these parts, but just the same lock the doors and don't go wandering off too far into the woods. Stick to the trails. And mind what I said 'bout the cellar."

"Okay, I will," she said and smiled again.

"I got me some fall clean-up to do here next week so I'll come by and check in on yah."

"Okay, and thanks for the ride."

He nodded and then drove off.

The daytime hours were all that she had hoped they would be, but at night the big house seemed a little too lonely and the beautiful countryside became a little too dark. It wasn't any wonder she had imagined the strange noises. The incident tonight was little more than her mind creating problems where none existed.

Nothing new there, she thought.

Satisfied with the explanation she prepared for bed. Of course, her rationalization did not extend to leaving her bedroom door unlocked, but as she turned the little thumb lock she argued that the action was for protection from the 'known' dangers of her secluded little world, not the supernatural ones that threatened to reveal themselves from the imaginative corners of her mind.

The next morning the sun warmed her bedroom in cheery shades of gold and amber and the previous night was all but forgotten. When she found her bedroom's door locked, it reminded her of what a scaredy cat she could be, and she shook her head and chuckled. She went downstairs, ate breakfast, read for a couple of hours, and finally dressed for a walk in the woods.

Autumn had reached its pinnacle and the trees were on fire with red, orange, and yellow leaves. Ashley walked into the forest and followed the well-worn hiking trails that surrounded the property. The air was fragrant and crisp and she became lost in her own thoughts. She found a less traveled path. It was narrower than the others were and the dying brush and tall grass encroached on all sides. The little dirt path wound deeper and deeper into the woods and the trees drew closer together. The canopy of leaves soon blocked out the sky and it wasn't until she reached a small clearing that she realized how low the sun had sunk toward the horizon.

The clearing consisted mostly of a large, still pond. The water looked black, but nothing about the smell suggested it was stagnant. Still, something about the dark water unnerved her. A part of her felt desperate to approach it and peer into its deep blackness. She found herself halfway to the water's edge before another part of her mind gained control of her legs and insisted she stop. She looked up at the sky and saw that dusk quickly approached.

My god, how long was I standing here, she wondered.

The shadows had grown long and the woods looked dark and foreboding. That other part of her mind continued to seduce her toward the pond, but she fought it and turned back for the house.

On the path, she picked up her speed and found it was all she could do not to break into a run. There was no reason to be afraid, it was not yet dark and there had been nothing in the woods to suggest danger. Still her active imagination tried to throw up images that Ashley forcefully ignored. Behind her, she heard twigs snapping and brush being pushed aside. She didn't look back, but decided that a little jog would be good for her legs. She ran the rest of the way to the house. Inside she closed and locked the doors as the sun set and darkness covered the countryside.

After dinner, she changed into her flannel pajamas and settled onto the large living room sofa with her book. She read until her eyes grew so tired that the words blurred. She stood, stretched, and decided to call it a night. She rechecked the doors and windows, turned off the downstairs lights, and then headed to the bed.

She made it only to the ninth step when she heard the footsteps behind her. They sounded wet and squishy the way the grass did when you walked on it after a heavy rain. Even with the light from the upper hallway, it felt like the darkness of the first floor pushed against her. She ran up the stairs and into her room. She closed the door, but this time did not wait to set the lock. She turned on the bedroom light and then slid down the door and rested against it.

She pressed her ear against the door and listened. On the other side, she heard the sound of breathing.

It's your own breath dummy, her mind argued.

She held her breath and listened. The sound was still there.

A wet raspy sound as something inhaled and exhaled.

The sound of the morning wind and rain woke her. Her neck and back were knotted and stiff. She had fallen asleep leaning against the door. She stood and stretched and her joints cracked and popped in relief. She shook her head and chastised herself for her foolishness. There was absolutely nothing in the house. How could she even think about surviving Grad school in New York City if she was too afraid to spend a night alone out here in the quiet country? She went to the large walk-in closet to put on her robe. She needed a hot shower to un-knot the muscles in her back.

The closet was enormous. It was almost larger than her dorm room at school. It was so big in fact, that it had its own window. Ashley found that to be strange. Her clothes hung on a small section of the closet pole and the Murphy's clothes, wrapped in their plastic garment bags filled the rest. The closet's back half was a dark space filled with boxes and old furniture. All those dark cubbies seemed the perfect hiding place for spiders and she shuddered at the thought. She put on her robe and returned to the bedroom door. She unlocked it and was not surprised to find that no one waited on the other side. She stepped into the carpeted hallway and her bare foot came down on a puddle of cold water. She leapt back into her room.

Impossible, she thought.

She made a closer inspection. There was a small puddle of water about the size of a basketball just outside the doorway. A step made in either direction and she would have missed it all together. The previous evening suddenly seemed very real until she heard the rain on the bedroom window.

"It's just a damn leak," she said to the quiet house. "I'll have to call Mr. Foster and let him know."

After her shower, she tried the old rotary phone on the kitchen wall. The wind must have knocked down the lines because there was no dial tone. She replaced the receiver on its hook and then returned to the little puddle of water. She used bath towels to soak up as much of the water as she could.

The cold rain kept her inside and she watched a few movies from the Murphy's DVD collection. She put the puddle and the imagined breathing out of her mind. The storm raged throughout the day and then into the night. At bedtime, she decided to combat her imagination head on. She did not intend to spend another night sleeping against the bedroom door.

She inspected all of the windows and doors locks. She looked in all the cabinets, opened, and inspected all the closets on the first floor. She looked behind and under all of the furniture until she was satisfied that nothing waited for her to turn off the lights. She went to the kitchen and poured herself some iced tea from the glass pitcher in the refrigerator. As she stood at the sink drinking, she heard a loud click from behind her. She turned and looked around. At first, she could see nothing that indicated its source. Then her eyes fell on the cellar door. It stood open just an inch.

It was locked. I know it was I just checked it.

She took a knife from the butcher's block and approached the door. She reached out slowly and placed her hand on the dark wood. She pushed hard and slammed the door closed. She grasped the old skeleton key that protruded from the lock. It took a couple of attempts before her shaking hand got it to turn and she heard the little steal bar lock into the frame.

Ashley stepped back and watched the door. Nothing happened. She approached and turned the handle. She pulled gently at first and then with more force. The door remained locked tight. She shook her head, finished her iced tea, and then put the glass in the sink.

"You are losing your shit," she said aloud and laughed.

She turned off the lights and went to the staircase.

She only made it to the seventh step when she heard the loud click from the kitchen. She froze on the stair and listened. The cellar door creaked open. A thick wet voice called her name. It sounded as if spoken through a mouthful of green and black stagnant water. The sound of it filled the quiet house.

Aaaagleeeee

Ashley ran up the stairs. In her bedroom, she locked the door and then barricaded it with the dresser. She spent most of the night curled up in the corner of her bed watching the door. Sometime later, she slept.

When she awoke the rain still fell and the wind howled at the window. She dressed quickly and moved the dresser from the doorway. As an afterthought, she went back to the closet. She had seen something there the other day and she desperately wanted it. She had an irrational fear that it would be gone, but when she opened the closet door, it was exactly where she had seen it. She picked up the old wooden baseball bat and carried it with her back to the bedroom door. She stepped into the hallway with the bat in hand and listened. The house was quiet except for the noisy voice of the wind. She went down the stairs and through the living room. She turned into the kitchen ready to face the open cellar door.

It was closed. She tested the handle. It was still locked. She picked up the phone and listened. The dial tone had returned. She thought about calling her parents, but dismissed the idea. What would she say?

Hi guys I'm a chicken shit and I want to abandon my responsibility to the Murphy's and come home.

That was crazy. She looked at the little card next to the phone. There, as promised was Mr. Foster's phone number. She could call him but again, what would she say?

I know you told me to stay away from the basement but I imagined the door opening so could you come over.

That qualified as crazy option number two.

She placed the receiver on its cradle and looked at the baseball bat. She leaned it against the wall. It was too stormy to walk into town, but maybe she could learn how to drive a stick shift. How hard could it be? The thought made her feel a little better. She needed a change of scene. She would give it a shot right after breakfast.

The truck started on the first try. She knew enough to depress the clutch and the rest she figured out after several practice runs in the driveway. She only stalled it a few times when she released the clutch too fast and didn't give it enough gas. When she felt confident that she wouldn't kill herself or anyone else she drove down the drive and headed for town.

The town was small but quaint. It had a general store where she bought a new book, some candy bars, and a hoodie that read, "I heart Spenceville." The town also had a little coffee shop. The aroma inside was delicious and the place felt warm and inviting. The interior boasted large overstuffed chairs and sofas. People came and went in small groups and Ashley found the sound of human interaction very welcoming after the lonely days and nights at the Murphy's.

She ordered coffee, settled into a big chair near the window, and read her book. The novel was actually quite good and she lost herself in it. The sounds of the shopkeepers closing up brought her back to reality. She looked at her watch and was surprised at how late the hour had grown. She thanked the owners and left the shop.

The ride back was uneventful, but when she arrived, it was nearly dark and the wind and rain had returned. She didn't want to track mud and water onto the oak floored foyer so she went around the back and entered through the kitchen door. She took off her muddy boots and wet jacket and left them by the door. She locked it and closed the curtains. She had drunk a lot of coffee and now really needed the bathroom. She turned towards the living room and stopped. The cellar door was open.

Her first instinct was to run, and then she remembered that Mr. Foster said he would be stopping by sometime during the week.

"That's it," she said to herself. "Mr. Foster came by and left the door open."

She looked for the baseball bat she had placed against the wall but it was gone.

Just further proof, she thought. He saw the bat and put it away.

She went to the cellar door and pushed it closed. She turned the key and locked it. She looked at the phone on the wall.

Well, it wouldn't hurt to check. Just to be sure, he stopped by. I mean a girl can't be too safe right?

She picked up the receiver and listened for the dial tone. It whined softly at her.

She read the numbers off Mr. Foster's card and her finger found the first digit. Before she dialed, the tone changed. It sounded like gurgling water. Someone whispered on the other end - Out of service the voice giggled.

Ashley dropped the receiver and fell back to the counter.

"No," she said aloud. "It's all in your damn head."

She forced herself back to the phone and picked up the dangling receiver. She placed it to her ear. There was no dial tone. She replaced it on its hook, went to the living room, and sat on the sofa.

For a long time, she considered her options.

I am not crazy, her mind insisted.

Are you sure? Another voice in her head asked.

Yes, she was certain. It was just stress. The break up with Mike, the tough final semester, and the financial aid issues that had delayed Grad school.

If you're not crazy, the voice asked, then is this all real?

Real? What's really happened? A wet carpet, an old cellar door that keeps popping open. Imagined sounds and voices. I'm making something out of nothing, that's all.

The little speech drew up her anger. She stood, went to the second floor, and turned on all the lights. Then she returned and turned on all the lights on the first floor. She made herself dinner and watched a movie. Whenever she caught herself thinking about the cellar door, she immediately put it out of her mind. She refused to check on it.

At bedtime, she shut off the television, but left all the lights on. She paused at the bottom of the stairs and took a deep breath. She would not run, no matter what she thought she heard. She took the first step and waited. Then she took a second and a third and each time she paused and listened. She did the same on each of the seventeen stairs until she had reached the top. She turned slowly and looked down the staircase. Nothing waited there. She was alone.

She went into her bedroom and closed the door. She considered the small lock, but then refused to secure it. She undressed, got into bed and after a moment's thought, she turned off the bedside lamp. The rain fell softly at the window and she started to drift off to sleep beneath the warm soft blankets.

Something behind the closet door giggled. Ashley heard the soft squeak as the closet's door handle turned.

She jumped out of the bed and ran from the room. She sprinted down the hallway and into the bathroom. She slammed and locked the door. She sat with her back against the toilet and cried for a long time. Finally, she pulled the towels from the linen closet and made a bed inside the tub. She laid in it and listened. The only sound was the wind and the rain. When the soft gray light of dawn filled the window, she fell asleep.

When she awoke the light at the window was weak and gray. She stood and stepped out of the tub. Her back was stiff and her head ached. She threw some water in her face and brushed her teeth. Then she left the bathroom. She went back to her bedroom and looked at the little digital clock on the nightstand. It was after four in the afternoon. She had slept for the entire day. She forced herself to open the closet. There was nothing there but clothes and the boxes and furniture. She checked the entire closet and then looked under her bed. Nothing.

She went downstairs. The cellar door was still closed and locked, but she didn't pick up the phone. All the lights were still on in the house and she left them. It would be dark again soon. She ate a peanut butter and jelly sandwich and some potato chips. She tried to read, but she couldn't concentrate on the words. Her mind worked furiously at a solution. She knew the answer, she just wanted to delay acceptance. She had to leave. Whether the sounds were imagined or real, she couldn't stay here any longer. The Murphy's would be pissed. Her parents would be disappointed, but that seemed insignificant compared to the fear that twisted inside of her. She wanted to leave today, but the last bus left Spenceville at five and there wasn't enough time to pack and then make the four mile walk to town. She would leave tomorrow. She could call Mr. Foster from the phone at the general store and ask him to watch the house until she could contact the Murphy's. At the first bus stop, she would call her parents and ask if she could stay with them for a few weeks.

When it was settled in her mind, she felt much better. She put her book down and surfed through the stations on the satellite television. Nothing held her interest and she began to drift off. She slept for a while and when she woke, she saw that the wall clock read eleven p.m. The rain had stopped but the wind still howled in the eaves and she could hear the sound of it rustling through the trees. The house was bright and warm. All the lights were still on and she wondered if the Murphy's would bitch her out when they got their next electric bill.

She decided to go to bed. She wanted to get up early and walk into town first thing in the morning. She would catch the earliest bus available. She turned off the television and got off the sofa. She figured that now that she had made her decision to leave, the noises and strange voices would bother her no further. It had all been in her head. The demons that haunted her weren't in this house, they were in her past.

She only made it to the fourth step when all the lights went out. A cold wet claw encircled her ankle. It pulled her off her feet. She reached out in the dark and tried to grab hold of the stair's banister. She missed it. The clawed hand yanked her down the stairs. She twisted over on her back as it pulled her through the living room. In the dark, she couldn't see the thing that gripped her ankle only the grotesque outline of its misshapen head. She could however see the open cellar door that it dragged her toward.

Ashley screamed.

The End.

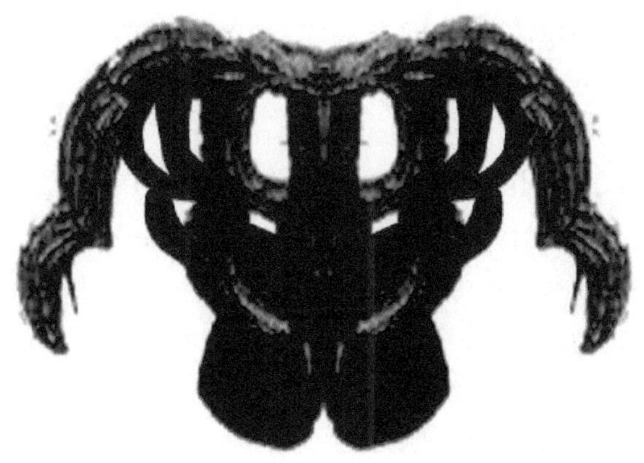

The Temporal Doorway by Faith Marlow

Anne sat huddled in the corner of her sofa, wrapped in a chenille blanket. She gazed blankly toward the coffee table, looking through it.

Her eyelids were heavy, closing slowly without her knowledge. Wrapped in the blanket like a huddled mummy, her long black hair spilled down her back and contrasted against the monochromatic color scheme of her house and furnishings, as if a careless writer had spilled a bottle of ink across a blank sheet of paper.

Maddie stood on the opposite side of the great room, frozen in her tracks as she left the kitchen. She could see Anne was balanced on the edge between sleep and awake and did not wish to startle her. The dreams had started, signifying the beginning of the inevitable visitations the Light Bringer had foretold. She had not given in to sleep in two days, knowing that the next time her eyes closed they could open to see the inside of an extraterrestrial laboratory where her hall closet had once been.

Stress and fatigue had taken their toll on Anne, physically, mentally, and professionally. She looked weathered, stretched thin. Her lustrous hair was dull, her complexion darkened, and her thin frame had lost several pounds since the events in New Mexico. Her patients had temporarily been referred to other doctors and her receptionist, Angie, had been given an extended vacation with full pay. Now all she could do was wait to be taken and hope for the best.

Anne's eyes finally closed and seconds later, her head dropped but immediately popped back up. Her eyes were wide, disoriented, stretching to open. "I'm awake." She said, spotting Maddie.

"You have to sleep. I told you I would watch you, won't even leave to go pee." Maddie lectured, sitting on the opposite end of the sofa.

"I know…" Anne sighed. "The dreams are getting worse. It's going to be soon. I can feel them watching me even when I'm awake." She confessed, rubbing her eyes. "They're not going to take their time with me like they did with Liz and Karen."

Maddie shifted uncomfortably, looking away from her.

"What is it, Maddie?" She instantly knew her friend was hiding something from her. Despite having known one another for only a few weeks, the women had developed a strong friendship, a loyalty, like soldiers in the trenches of war. "Somebody found Karen, didn't they?" Maddie nodded in agreement. Anne impatiently waited for her to divulge the details. "Well…"

"Karen was found about ten miles from her house in the middle of a field by a man and his son who were searching for their lost dog, a lot like Liz." Maddie said, almost whispering.

"Two of her ex-husbands are being investigated as "persons of interests" in the case, since the dogs were missing."

"Anything about the house?"

"No. Police say it was burned to destroy evidence, that she was killed there and dumped. No word about a little body inside."

"What if one of those men go to prison for this? We have to say something to the police." Anne said, flustered by the possibility of a wrongly accused innocent.

"And say what, that Karen was abducted and murdered by aliens?" Maddie said, a hint of sarcasm to regain Anne's focus. Sleep deprivation had skewed her usually sound logic. The topic had become such a normal part of their lives that it was often a difficult realization that the rest of the population still believed extraterrestrials and abductions were the work of Hollywood and those desperate for attention.

"Yeah… I would hate for someone to think I was crazy, could be bad for my career." Anne's face went blank, as devoid emotion as a porcelain doll. "I don't think I will have to worry about my career much longer."

"Anne, the Light Bearer told you that you would be okay." "Really? How do I know that was even real? I could have just been dreaming. I don't feel any different. I don't look any different. Maybe I just wanted hope, so my mind created it." Anne's raw emotions were beginning to unravel, her eyes filled to the brim with tears that stung her bloodshot eyes.

"You don't believe that. What about that little bastard at Karen's house that had me floating a foot off the ground? Was that a figment of your imagination?"

Anne rubbed her eyes. "I know… it's the waiting that's killing me."

"Sleep. Please. I am right here."

"Not yet." Anne drew in a deep breath and clenched her jaw. "Tonight I want to be so tired that I have no other choice than fall asleep. I don't want to lay there thinking about it. I am tired, done putting it off. Do it for Liz and Karen, and for Ashley, right?"

"No Anne, no one can help them now." Maddie said, squeezing Anne's hand, looking her straight in the eye. She always meant business when she looked a person in the eye, her words directly from her heart. "End it for you, and so no other girl will ever have to go through this again."

***

Anne chose her favorite pajamas to wear to bed, baby blue silk. She wanted to be covered, buttoned up. She tried not to think about Liz, Karen, and young Ashley, their nude bodies dumped like processed carcasses.

"Goodnight, Anne." Maddie said wistfully. She wished she could tell her something more comforting but the words escaped her.

"Goodnight, Maddie." Anne said, biting her lip at the end. "If you hear anything, just stay in your room. Don't come out."

"But…"

"No." Anne stood firm. "Don't draw attention to yourself. Stay quiet. I'll be okay."

Maddie nodded hesitantly and closed her door. Anne sighed and climbed into bed, quickly followed by Elliot. He quickly curled up in his favorite spot, snuggled against the small of her back. Her head on her pillow and linens pulled to her chin, she willfully closed her eyes for the first time in over fifty hours. Almost instantly she felt as though she was falling into thick, padded darkness, as if the mattress was miles deep. Sleep would come quickly.

The acrid smell of chemicals and disinfectants settled in the back of Anne's throat, stirring her from her sleep yet still unable to open her eyes. She could taste the smell, her mouth dry. She wanted to swallow but lacked the moisture. The hum of machinery reminded her drowsy mind of the fountain on her nightstand, but as she became more and more aware, she knew she was no longer in her bed or even her bedroom. She opened her eyes and gasped, blinding white light overtaking her vision. She looked around frantically to see anything, but her eyes were unable to focus, overexposed. She had been taken.

"Who's there?" She wanted to shout out, but her parched throat would not allow more than a crackling whisper. She squinted tightly and tried to get her bearings. The walls and ceiling appeared to be rounded, like a dome. A rounded shield of shiny mental, like highly polished aluminum, focused the large light directly over her head. For the first time since waking, she tried to move her arms but tight restraints at her wrists prevented her from doing so. Her legs were the same, bound at the ankles. She wanted to scream, plead for her release but she remembered the Light Bringer's gentle words and calm presence. She choked down the fear and the stale taste in her mouth and pretended to be more sedated than she actually was, and waited.

She looked through her eyelashes, watching the creatures as they scurried around her. Luckily for her, they had not taken out her contacts, at least not yet. There were four, as best she could count. They were identical in size, weight, color and age. Like worker ants, they hurried between their machines, changing the readouts by pressing characters she could not recognize on touch screens. One individual walked close to her, leaning its flat, emotionless face close to hers. Its skin was grayish green, like a corpse, black shark eyes that only rarely blinked. She could feel its breath on her face as it inspected her. Her heart rate began to accelerate and she bit her tongue to suppress a scream, desperately trying to stay calm. The small being jumped back, as if it had been offended, almost scared, but the lack of facial expression made it impossible to be certain. It began to chatter earnestly, keeping its distance. Anne faintly tasted blood, the tip of her tongue tender. She wondered what it meant, if there was a connection.

The beings communicated with one another with more clicks and chatters of different pitches and volumes, circling her, back and forth to the machines. Then three approached her together, one went to each arm and the third by her head. Elongated fingers with fleshy tips instead of fingernails, resembling the suckers of an octopus, grasped her head. It palmed her head like an enormous basketball player would the ball, turning it to expose the left side of her neck. She felt a cold metallic halo being strapped against her head, clicking into place in a slot in the table. Anne gritted her teeth and refused to show fear, refused to give them the pleasure of knowing she was terrified. She felt three simultaneous flashes of pain as the intravenous lines were introduced into her veins and were immediately followed by searing heat passing fluidly throughout her body.

Anne could hide the pain no longer and a wild, animal-like, scream erupted from her. She drew in a ragged breath, only to scream once more, eyes wide open and staring spitefully at the creature by her head.

"Let me go, you little bastard!" She growled, calling it by Maddie's favorite name for them. She struggled violently against the restraints, despite feeling the metal cuffs chaffing into her skin. The entire table shook as Anne raged against her captors, until the cold metal box she had read of in Liz's journal was locked into place over her abdomen.

"No! No! Get that thing away from me, you little shit!" She screamed, realizing she had never cursed so much in her life. The ominous box that she could only see from the corner of her eye began to hum and two probes quickly descended and stabbed into her abdomen, straight through into her ovaries. Anne howled with pain, her back arching from the table despite the restraints. The machine's sound changed with its function, unleashing another wave of pain into her body. The probes retracted and the humming changed pitch again as it processed the material it had harvested. Blood bubbled out of the incisions, hot running down the chilled flesh of her hips. "I'm going to kill you, you little bastard! You hear me? I'll kill you when I get loose!"

Anne panted for breath, light headed and fatigued from pain and fear. The creatures chattered feverishly, checking screens, checking machines, prying her eyes open to see if she had passed out. She wondered if the procedures were over, if she had indeed survived like the Light Bringer had promised. Her guard faltered for just a moment and she was rewarded with an instrument being introduced into her navel, lightning fast and wicked sharp. She gasped, unable to speak as she endured the perfect example of pain. The machine changed functions again and she felt heat, like a volcanic rock had been injected into her belly. Despite the white-hot light, the edges of her peripheral vision began to darken and she knew she was blacking out, but helpless to stop it. Helpless.

***

Anne's spirit floated in soothing, healing darkness. She did not know where she was, if she was anywhere, but she had been freed from the torment of her body and in that moment, it was enough. In the distance, she could see a familiar sight, the comforting blue of the Light Bringer. She willed herself toward it, hoping the gentle face from her dream would be waiting for her.

"There you are, little one." The nebulous glow seemed to bloom, unfurling and releasing the benevolent extraterrestrial, the birth of a much different Venus than Botticelli had envisioned.

"Am I dead?" Anne asked naively, unsure of anything after what she had experienced.

"Dead?" The being was puzzled by her question, by the idea of death. "No, your body is still functional, battered but not broken, little one. You survived and now you are ready to fulfill your task."

Anne felt like she was being pulled by a rope around her waist, effortlessly racing away from the light. "Wait!"

Maddie lay in bed, her hands over her ears, eyes tightly closed. Gertie was barking insanely at the bedroom door, scratching, growling, and turning circles. Anne's last words to her had been to stay still, be invisible. She felt spineless, allowing Anne's words to soothe her fears, to accept inaction. Gertie was gnawing at the bottom of the door. Maddie wadded her fists and set her jaw. She leapt to her feet, flung open her bedroom door and charged toward Anne's room, valiant Gertie just ahead of her. She grabbed the knob but it refused to turn. She could hear Elliot and Michael barking like the room was on fire.

"Anne!" Maddie screamed, bashing the door with her shoulder, again and again, until she broke the lock free from the jamb. Gertie charged in fearlessly, her human companion right behind her, but they stopped in their tracks. Save the two terrified dogs, the room was empty. The fountain trickled on Anne's nightstand, her powder blue pajamas in a pile on the floor.

"Dammit!" Maddie bellowed to the ceiling, sending the dogs running out of the room. "You were supposed to protect her!"

She wanted to punch someone, wanted to curse until she was blue in the face, wanted to walk right into that light and bring her friend back, but she was powerless. The light had disappeared and it had taken Anne with it.

She picked up the pajamas from the floor, looking them over for any sign that Anne had been injured or struggle but there was nothing, not even a peculiar smell. Defeated and ashamed, Maddie sat on the edge of Anne's bed and neatly folded her pajamas before placing them on her pillow. All she could do was wait and hope.

***

Groggy and sore, Anne opened her eyes, unsure if she had been unconscious for hours or days. She was in complete darkness, folded into a fetal position, tightly surrounded on all sides, encapsulated. Her fingers desperately searched for an opening, fearing that every breath she drew in would be the last one contained within her cocoon. The strong, synthetic material was impossible to tear or puncture with her fingernails but with effort, she was able to find the opening that had been sealed after she had been stuffed inside. She pushed one hand through first, and then the other, able to stretch the opening far enough for her shoulders. She struggled, crawling like an insect as her wounded abdomen screamed with every inch. Finally liberated, she attempted to stand but her incisions refused to allow her to straighten her back.

Nude and hunched over, holding her midsection, she looked around the room. Multiple pods made of the same material filled the floor, piled haphazardly like trash on the curb. She could see no movement, could detect no sign of life. She spotted a door on the opposite side of the room and shambled toward it, taking twice as long for her to cover the distance as it should. A small screen similar to the ones she had noticed on the machines in the laboratory was on the door. The characters that had then seemed foreign to her now looked strangely familiar. With a trembling finger, she hesitantly touched a symbol and the door lifted silently, revealing an unattended hallway.

Anne found that she could only take a few steps before the pain overwhelmed her and forced her to lean against the wall. Her mind was dizzy with questions, clueless to her location or the direction she needed to be moving in, but she trudged forward. Which way might lead to safety, which way led to danger? Which door, if any, would lead her back home?

Ahead of her, she could see the intense light of the laboratory shining through a tiny porthole sized window. She stumbled forward, gritting her teeth as she thought of her child-sized captors and their torturous procedures. She thought of Karen the pariah, of despondent Liz and her own failure to save her, of unfortunate Ashley, who was robbed of her future, and of Maddie, so haunted by her past that she felt guilty for living. Lives shattered, families broken, all without consequence until that night in New Mexico, finally a life for a life.

Activating another touch screen, the door to the laboratory opened but Anne backed against the wall, waiting for one of the beings to walk out into the hall to investigate. The door slid closed again with no sign of her assailants. She touched the symbol again, the door slid back up and she crept inside, quickly crouching beside a tall machine. She listened, holding her breath, for any sound of movement, clicking chatter, or functioning machines but heard nothing but the quiet hum of equipment in standby mode.

The acrid cleaner smell had diminished but was replaced by a foul, rotten smell. She tiptoed around the room, getting closer and closer to the source of the odor. As she cautiously approached the table where her procedures had taken place, she saw three of the beings sprawled on the ground, lifelessly wheezing. Their smooth skin was now mottled with sores that seemed to darken and expand before her eyes. She could see the substance that was their blood seeping from their slit-like nostrils and from the corners of their mouths and eyes. The closer she got to these dying creatures, the more their condition deteriorated. Away from the others, the fourth was dragging itself toward a bank of touch screens and panels.

She walked past the three like an angel of death, expiring in her wake. Their fragile bodies immediately began to bloat, burst, and decompose into puddles of thick, black sludge. When the fourth saw her approach, it screeched in terror. It sounded like it had pneumonia, its chest filled with mucous. It pulled itself up on the console and pointed its middle, longest finger toward a flashing icon on one of the screens. Before it could make contact, Anne grabbed it by the ankle and pulled it away from the console. The creature screamed, grasping weakly at the ground to pull away. When she released its ankle, the disintegrating flesh sloughed off its leg and hung off her hand, sticky with her own blood.

"I want to go home!" She shouted, grabbing the being by the shoulders and shaking it. It howled pitifully, congestion in its chest increasing as her fingers melted into its flesh. "How do I get home?" A quiet hiss escaped the being's small mouth and its eyes immediately hazed over. Anne jumped back as its body began to liquefy. Its enormous skull with cavernous eye sockets was the last to dissolve, staring at her from the black puddle.

Anne looked at the console, bewildered. She was afraid to touch any of the symbols. There were too many to trust a whim. Defeated and exhausted, she slumped to the floor and crawled into the gap between two machines, staring out at the carnage around her. It was impossible for her to be any more alone. She looked around, hoping to find something to cover herself with but saw nothing in the sterile laboratory. She pulled her legs close to her chest and laid her head on her knees, fatigue and blood loss finally taking their toll. She closed her eyes and allowed sleep to pull her under with no hope of waking again.

***

Maddie dozed at the foot of Anne's bed, unaware that she had even fallen asleep. The closet doorway began to flutter with a film of blue light, developing around the frame and pulling inward toward the center of the space. Instantly Anne's designer clothes and shoes disappeared behind the glow and the Light Bringer stepped into room in the flesh. Her graceful, elongated body floated with easy grace, her tiny feet barely making a sound on the hardwood flooring. She saw the sleeping young woman and smiled, like a mother gazing at her sleeping child. She bent at the waist, her slender legs and backward facing knees crouching so she could touch Maddie's cheek. Her eyes popped open, instantly terrified. She screamed and began to back pedal across the bed away from her. Her three tiny bodyguards first considered barking but instead huddled around her at the headboard.

Maddie wanted to speak but she could only shake and stutter, her eyes wide and refusing to blink. "Wha…wha…what d…d…do" She desperately tried to speak but awe had stolen her words.

"Do not fear me, little one." The being spoke, her long arms outstretched like she was going to embrace her. "Are you prepared to help your friend? She will need you soon."

"Yes." She answered bravely without question, without hesitation. "So fragile, yet so brave." The Light Bringer whispered, extending her lengthy hand to Maddie. "Such an honorable species."

Anne was awakened suddenly to the violent shuddering of the substructure beneath her. She instantly realized how oblivious she had been to her location, how many floors were beneath or above her, if she was on a craft adrift in space or in a structure on some distant world unknown to human scientists. Alarms began to sound. Flashing lights on the consoles alerted the causes. Anne pushed herself up and grimaced, a hot knife of pain sliced across her abdomen and a thick drop of blood belched from her navel. The floor shook again, reverberating into the walls and up her legs. Anne searched desperately for anything she could use as a weapon, anything to protect herself from whatever threatened her from below. The glint of shiny metal caught her eye. She shuffled across the room and grabbed a scalpel- like knife from a small table and hid beneath a console bank as far from the door as she could get.

From the hallway, she could hear movement approaching, an army by the sound of it. Anne could feel her insides trembling. Never in a thousand years, not even in her wildest dreams, could she have imagined this would be how the last moments of her life would be spent. The door opened silently and a rush of grey soldiers poured in. Like rats escaping a flood, the beings filed into the room. They filled the space orderly, those in front allowing room for the ones in back, as if they were all being controlled by a single consciousness. Their huge, black almond eyes stared in her direction, emotionless, ruthless. The last being to enter the room was twice as tall as the others, roughly the same as Anne. Resembling the Light Bringer more than the others, this lanky being appeared to be controlling the others. They looked where it looked, moved like an extension of it.

Anne rose and stood brave, straight back, ignoring the pain in her belly to defiantly stare her death in the eye. The Dark One pointed its finger at her and she was instantly aware of it within her mind, speaking to her without the need of language or speech.

"You are the speck of dust that destroyed one of mine." It said, its message unfurling within Anne's mind like the blackest storm clouds. "Yes, and these." She responded smugly. The being scowled and clenched its extended hand into a fist. Anne screamed, clutching the sides of her head. It felt as though her skull was being hammered on all sides simultaneously. She fell to her knees, blood dripping from her nose.

The soldiers gasped and Anne could see, despite her blurred vision, they collectively held their throats, coughed and gagged. The Dark One seemed confused and the grip on Anne's mind lessened.

Ashley. Liz. Karen. Maddie.

"Not again." Anne whispered. Adrenaline overwhelmed her and she seized the opportunity. She quickly slashed into her left arm with the scalpel before the Dark One became aware of her intentions. Blood flowed effortlessly from the gash that stretched from elbow to wrist, filling the entire room with the scent of metallic death, theirs and hers. She took the scalpel in her left hand and gripped it as tightly as her injured ligaments and muscles would allow. She quickly pulled her other wrist across the ultra sharp edge, amazed that for a split second there was no pain. But in an instant she began to feel it burn, feel the pucker of flesh separating and sealing together with the turn of her wrist, blood percolating through the crack. The knife fell from her hand, which was now coated and slick with blood, having served its purpose. She had fulfilled her purpose.

Anne's legs collapsed beneath her, her lip quivered and tears filled her eyes despite her determination to remain brave. She knew death was coming, could feel it slipping over her like a cold embrace of winter wind. Looking down at her self- wrought carnage, she could faintly see tiny blue particles floating away from her, like her wounds were expelling pollen. The soldier creatures began to wane, sores forming on their skin. They coughed and gurgled, falling to the ground independently as the Dark One's control over them weakened.

As its army sank into ruin and sores began to develop across its body, the Dark One looked at Anne with a hateful, disbelieving stare.

"How?" It asked, using the last of its energy to push one last question into her mind. Anne smiled, knowing it would die without an answer. She fell back, looked up to the ceiling and laughed. She didn't know either.

A vibrant blue light outlined the door of the laboratory. Again the light filled in the doorway, like a bubble, and thickened in consistency until the temporal doorway was completed. A pair of dirty Converse sneakers tiptoed through the pool of thick, melted alien waste. Maddie saw Anne across the room, surrounded in a puddle of blood and sludge.

"Anne!" She shook her shoulders, tapped her face. Her partially opened eyes stared blankly, her lips blue, body cold. "We're too late! She's already dead!" Maddie shouted, looking back at the doorway. "Dammit!"

Maddie quieted and cocked her head, listening to the voice in her head, the Light Bringer. She locked her arms under Anne's armpits and pulled her toward the door, her heels dragging tracks through the black sludge. The doorway quickly closed behind them, closing the link between the two worlds for the last time.

***

Two Weeks Later

Maddie stood in the middle of the serenity garden, holding the biodegradable urn gingerly. The sapling would be nourished by her ashes, a silent, resilient memorial.

"You think she would like this?"

"I do. Liz always loved this garden." Anne answered, joining her. She rubbed at her bandages. The healing wounds itched. "For a moment, I thought you would be planting two trees out here."

"When the Light Bringer opened the doorway and I found you, you were already cold. You were dead, not to mention lying in a pool of alien ooze. That was disgusting. You owe me, washing that shit off you." Maddie smirked playfully.

Anne put her arm around her shoulder and pulled her close. "Yes I do. Thank you, Maddie. The Light Bringer would not have been able to revive me otherwise. They were poisonous to one another, light and dark. That's why she needed me. She needed a vehicle."

Together the women placed the urn in the ground, covered and watered it. "I just wish it had been in time to save Liz, and Karen." Anne said, staring down at the sapling. She already looked tired. "Ashley never had a chance."

"You can't think of it like that." Maddie reassured, leading her back inside. She didn't want Anne to overdo herself, get too stressed out. "Thanks to you, no one else will have to lose their sister, or anyone else. Anne the alien slayer. Joss Whedon might make a show about you."

"Who?"

"You're hopeless."

Anne stretched out on the patient's couch, looking back out the window as she rested, distant.

"You okay?" Maddie asked. She seemed pale, dark under her eyes. Her recovery had been slow.

Anne rubbed her stomach, still tender from the incisions. She recalled the white hot injection she had received through her navel but kept it to herself. She smiled, hoping to put her friend's mind at ease. "I'm fine, just a little sick at my stomach. Think I stood up too fast."

A couple more weeks and she would know for certain, one way or the other, if her suspicions were true.

The End

Zombie Apocalypse Now! by Rachel
Tsoumbakos

CASE ONGOING

And What of Pippa?

The problem with being this far from the teller's stalls was the lack of a stabbing implement, such as a pen.

Pippa writhed and kicked at the zombie that had her ankle. This one was a new one and not the woman from behind the glass. She must have been killed properly the second time her head hit the glass.

This new zombie had much more grunt to him. He was big and fat. His grey guts wobbled as they protruded from the bottom of his torn shirt. The mottled skin reminded Pippa of a dead seal she'd seen once at the beach. He smelled about the same too.

Kicking fiercely, she actually made contact with the dead man's nose. A squelch and the splintering of bones could be heard. The blow wasn't hard enough to be fatal though. She'd have to come up with something else.

While the surprise of a broken nose distracted the zombie momentarily, it still wasn't enough for her to wriggle free from his vice-like grip. Her long skirt had ridden up around her knees as she'd fallen and it was now tangling with the fat zombie, making the situation more confusing.

Frantically, Pippa reached out and clawed at the ground. Her fingers clasped at brochures and random bits of tattered paper, but nothing more substantial.

A banjo played in the distance.

A banjo?

Pippa questioned her sanity. Was this really the end? A growl bubbled up from deep in her chest and she rolled herself upwards. Her baby bump prevented her from sitting up properly, but at least she could now prop herself up while still batting at the grotesque man. She looked around for anything that might work to get her away from the zombie.

Paper, paper, everywhere!

Shit!

And then she spied something glinting at her from between two sheets of paper on the ground to her left.

It was her only hope.

She kicked once more at the zombie and managed to poke her sandaled toe into the obese zombie's eye. There was a squirt of eye fluid and a roar from the zombie. Bile rose in her throat and she vomited.

Damn being pregnant and her weak stomach!

Surprisingly, the smell of vomit distracted the zombie. His nostrils flared and his looked away from Pippa, following his nose. There was a look of doubt on his face – if zombies could even *have* facial expressions. She knew it wouldn't be long before his realised his mistake and turned back to the real prize.

Rubbing harshly at her chin, she took her one golden opportunity and lurched sideways; reaching for the item she'd seen briefly before their frantic movement had moved everything. Her hand slapped down three or four times. Her legs kicked out with the ferocity only the undead can evoke and the small little baby in her stomach rolled about all over the place, thankful that it was safely protected by amniotic fluid and strong walls of muscles.

"Where are you?" she cried.

Off in the distance was the faint sound of a scream. Or was it the screech of car tyres? Pippa didn't have time to wonder about it.

Another slap as her hand felt nothing but paper and floor beneath it. Pulling both her legs towards her, she pushed with all her might against the zombie's head, trying desperately to keep his nasty teeth from her delicate flesh.

"I'm pregnant you fucker!" she screamed. Like he even cared. Could the undead still understand their native tongue?

Her hands splayed out and searched some more as her head hit the bank door. A ringing started in her ears and black spots danced in front of her eyes. It wasn't time to black out now! The door moved under her weight, but not by much.

The chains through the door handles prevented it.

The movement bought her closer to the *thing*. With renewed energy, she stretched out. There was a pop and a deep burn in her side, but she couldn't think about torn muscles just now for her hand had finally closed on the item.

Hopefully it was useful.

The zombie was now snapping at her ankles. His fetid teeth clicked and crunched together. Spit flew out of his mouth and splattered against her feet. Her stomach rolled again. She gulped and swallowed, not wanting to throw up again.

Her hand yanked at the item and bought it up in front of her face.

It was a key - probably the one that opened the chains on the door.

If she was lucky.

With the last vestige of strength left, Pippa lunged at the zombie. She wasn't sure if the key was long enough to do much damage, so she aimed for his popped eye.

She missed and got him in his flabby cheek. The zombie howled but more with fury than agony. She pulled back again.

Thirty-seven stabs later, Pippa rolled the finally dead zombie off her and sat up.

Gasping and wheezing, she clutched at her stomach and hugged at her unborn child, hoping against hope that it had not been injured in the attack. Her arms felt like jelly and the key jangled out of her fingers and clattered against the hard tiles of the bank's front entrance.

"Hey baby, mamma's okay." *But for how long?*

The fat zombie still clutched her ankle and the circulation was starting to falter. Reaching forward, she and loosened his grip. Only one finger was lost during the process. Pippa, unfortunately, lost her lunch again.

As she sat up, she noticed the revolver. So, the fat man was once a security guard. She removed the gun and its holster too, strapping it around her own growing belly.

Wiping one shaking hand across her forehead, she leaned back against the sturdy glass door. She couldn't help the tears as they flowed. Her breath sucked in great gulping sobs and she let herself be lost for a while.

A sharp sting to her thigh bought her out of her grief quickly.

The female was back!

She'd dragged herself silently across the floor while the fat zombie had her distracted. The broken leg had prevented her from getting at Pippa's brains. The bite would have the same effect though – it would just be a slower process.

"No," she screamed and fumbled for the key once more. She grabbed it quickly this time and killed the female zombie much quicker than the first.

It still didn't undo the damage.

Pippa jumped up and staggered as the pain in her side reminded her of her torn ligaments.

She had to act fast. Staggering through the bank, clutching at her side, she weaved her way through the teller area and through the big door that was held open with the pamphlet stand. She yanked it aside and pulled the door closed behind her.

Her heart hammered in her chest as she made her way down the narrow corridor and towards the staff room at the back. There was a first aid kit there and, surprisingly, running water.

She rushed as fast as her damaged muscles would allow and was tucked safely in the staff room within moments. Her muscles fought against her as she dragged a table across the door. It was heavy and therefore wasn't much, but a warning was better than another bite.

She ripped open the cupboard over the microwave and pulled out the meagre first aid supplies. Throwing the Band-Aids aside, she reached for the Betadine and haphazardly set it down on the little sink in the kitchenette.

The water was slightly muddy as it started to run before clearing over time. In her travels, Pippa had discovered a large water tank on the roof of this building that collected and stored water from the gutters. With the lack of electricity, the pump didn't work anymore but gravity still did its job.

Pulling a chair over, she climbed up and laid her leg in the sink. A few short months ago and she would not have to use the chair. Alas, it was probably time to say goodbye to her dancer's physique. And her free will. *When would the zombie gene kick in?*

She didn't know how long it would take, but she was ready to try anything to prolong her life. Pulling out a set of tweezers and a scalpel, she set to work.

At least there was nothing more in her grumbling stomach to throw up, although her gag reflex still worked. The poor baby inside her stomach felt a sharp contraction every time its mother heaved.

First, she washed the wound. That was the easy part.

Using the scalpel to remove all the flesh that had come in contact with the zombie's teeth was more torturous. Still, she scraped and dug at her thigh. The blood ran freely and sometimes she would have to stop, turn on the tap and clean the wound.

There was nothing in the kit that would aid her in sewing up the gaping wound, so she had to improvise. Pulling off her top, she checked it for signs of zombie blood.

It was spattered with the darn stuff!

So was her skirt.

She searched the room for anything she could use. Pulling her leg out of the sink, she tested its weight and cried out in pain as a result. Dragging the chair with her, she used it as a crutch and dragged it across the room as she hopped along with it. Blood gushed out and she was beginning to feel light-headed.

Still, she managed to reach the staff closet. There wasn't much inside, but after riffling around, she came across a long-discarded cardigan. The thin black thread would work, she decided.

She tried not to look at her blood trail as she made her way back to the sink.

She was not prepared for the agony of stitching her own flesh. Probably no one bar Chuck Norris would be. Clenching her teeth together, she suffering on; screaming with each incision. She didn't have a needle to thread the cotton onto, so she had to poke holes in her own flesh and then push the thread through with the tweezers. It was slow, sickening work.

Eventually it was done. She was proud of herself for not fainting. Finally she poured the entire contents of Betadine over her handy work.

She'd done everything she could think of.

Covering her wound with a bandage, she limped out the door. Slowly, she made her way to the front door, the key held tightly in her hands. Shaking with the shock of being bitten and then having to perform surgery on herself, she dropped it several times before managing to slide it into the padlock.

The click of freedom was loud in her ears as she exited the bank; her tomb.

The street was barren as she turned the corner and came face to face with three women and a cat.

Diary of Pippa Roscoe to her unborn child

January 23rd
(42 days after the first reported outbreak)

I got bitten today.

I also met people – finally.

They were hostile at first; one was pointing a spear gun at the other two. If I didn't have the gun I wouldn't have approached them. But I needed to be with people, little one. I needed someone to be there when I turned, so they could do what they had to do. The thought of you, my little baby, being alive inside of me and your mamma nothing but a mindless zombie, spurred me on.

Not telling them I'd been bitten was my own selfishness.

I guess I just want a few more hours with you little one.

And maybe I got to the wound quick enough. There is always hope, I guess…

Love always,
Mamma Pippa.

Will Tatiana, Rosalyn and Berta find out about Pippa's bite? Find out in Part 8 of Zombie Apocalypse Now!

Bestselling Horror US

1 — Better Off Dead in Deadwood - *A Charles & C.S. Kunkle*

2 *Seduced by Pain* - *Kimberly Kinrade*

3 Out Of Darkness (The Starborn Saga) - *Jason D. Morrow*

4 Zombie Patrol (Walking Plague Trilogy #1) - *J.R. Rain and Elizabeth Basque*

5 *The Sixth Extinction: An Apocalyptic Tale of Survival.* - *Glen Johnson*

6 *413* - *Rick Murcer*

7 Devil's Briar: The Complete Series - *Amy Cross*

8 Darkbound - *Michaelbrent Collings*

9 Exodus (The Little Seer) - *Laura Cowan*

10 Dream a Little Dream - *Antoinette Stockenberg*

Compiled Feb 1st - Feb 28th 2013
Amazon.com Kindle Chart

Bestselling Horror UK

1   Devil's Briar: The Complete Series - *Amy Cross*

2   Falling off the Bones - *Ian Woodhead*

3   Zombie Armageddon 5: Dead Reaping - *Ian Woodhead*

4   Beneath - *Kit Tinsley*

5   Zombie Armageddon:4 Dead Veil - *Ian Woodhead*

6   Bad Jack - *Adam Moon*

7   R'hela (The Bwy Hir Trilogy) - *Lowri Thomas*

8   The Shadows and the Darkness - *S.J. Byard*

9   Never Say Never - *Avionne Celestin*

10   Nana's House (Don't Dare Call Them Zombies) - *Zachary Stone*

Compiled Feb 1st - Feb 28th 2013
Amazon.co.uk Kindle Chart

On the.
Record

A Moment With Mark Tufo

I would like to introduce the writer of the Zombie Fallout series and The Indian Hill Trilogy amongst others, he is Mark Tufo.

Hi Barry, thank you for the interview it's great to be here!

What was your first experience of the horror genre?

The first written experience with horror was the Great One's, IT. Stephen King scared the hell out of me with that book and from there I couldn't get enough.

While you were growing up did you have a favourite genre of horror, or to put it another way when did your love affair with zombies begin?

I've related this story before but I fell in love with zombies at the tender age of 7 when my babysitting cousin thought watching The Night of The Living Dead might be a good way to while away our time. I'd never been quite so enthralled and petrified at the same time.

When you started to writing back in college did you send any of your work out to agents or publishers before going the self-publishing route?

I started writing my first book in college, I finished it 15 years later, at that point my wife and I sent it to every literary address we could find. I might have even sent a copy to the Library of Congress.

It's well documented that rejection is part of the writing process. If you do get a rejection letter, how do you process it before moving on?

Well rejection is always difficult, whether it's trying to get a date with Susan Collins in the fifth grade or trying to get a book published. I knew getting a publisher to look was a big stretch I mean not as much as getting a date with Susan but still a stretch. I'm being honest that yeah it was a bummer as rejection letter after letter kept rolling in but honestly my expectations were low. I thought our chances of success were minimal.

What are your pet peeves when it comes to reading other writers work?

To every writer their own style, I guess the only thing that really gets me is when they take the easy road out. There are times when I really will get my characters in a jam, one in which it'll sometimes take me three days trying to figure out how they will get out of it. I always try to make how they succeed as believable within the context of the story as possible. I've read stories where the author has his characters just stumble upon rocket launchers in a Wendy's or a comet streaks from the sky and BOOM all the bad guys are dead. It's just TOO convenient and a cop-out in my eyes.

With your success within the self-published market do you think there is still room for new writers?

Hell yeah there's always more room, I believe within the last six months it has got a little more difficult for writers to break through due to some policy changes from some of the distributors. But if you have a good, well written story readers will find you.

Your series Zombie Fallout has been picked up by Illuminandi Media for them to produce a film. How did that come about?

I had a reader/fan said he knew a producer and that he'd get us in touch. I thanked him but honestly I didn't put too much stock in it. Two weeks later I was on a three way call with two of the producers. It was a surreal moment.

Do you find your readers craving more that you can write? If so, how do you deal with that pressure?

From the first word I write to my wife hitting upload on amazon, B&N, Kobo, iBooks wherever, it's roughly a3.13 six-month process to get a book out. I'll get folks the day after launch asking when the next book will be available, I love the enthusiasm I do, I'm just not sure they realize how many steps go into that book. There's the initial write, then a re-read, re-write, then off to the editor where it gets crucified then back to me for re-writes. Then off to beta-readers for opinions and then more re-writes and finally formatting and uploading. At that point I would love to sit back and enjoy the completion of the endeavour for a couple of weeks, unfortunately I'm self-employed and my boss is an ass. I will generally take the day after launch off completely and then back to work the following day.

Along with other writers, you have a great presence on Facebook. You always seem to make time to answer your readers' question and set competitions for them. How important do you think social media is for a writer, and where do you draw the line regarding privacy?

Facebook and Twitter have been huge for me. I grew up in a blue collar family where manners were important. If someone takes the time out of their day to communicate with me then I feel obligated to do the same (plus it's cool as hell that folks want to say HI) that was never a marketing ploy just a basic courtesy on my part. I've been fairly lucky in the privacy department, that isn't to say there hasn't been a few line crossers but suffice it to say if you plan on being in the public eye, have a private and a public page, avoid any trouble before it happens.

With so much writing that you do, how do you find the time? Do you have a set routine that you stick to?

I used to write 7 days a week, in fact I felt compelled too. I have since decided to take Sundays off and try to rein my sanity back in. Not always successfully I might add. Finding the time is easy, I work from home, that is definitely a perk of this occupation.

You have been interviewed many times regarding your love of zombie fiction. Is there a question that you never been asked but you have a killer answer to?

This is a tough one, so much of my life is public knowledge at this point, so much so that my Unfair Contests of the Day which ask seemingly obscure questions about myself rarely go for longer than ten minutes any more. Killer answer, so I'm supposed to say something witty (see how I'm stalling?) Fine, I've never been asked what I would be like if I had fallen in love with Widespread Panic ten years sooner. I'D

BE *UCKED. I would have toured with them and I guarantee have burnt my mind to toasty bits by this time in my life. It would have been a hell of a ride though!

Can you tell us a little about the next book you have planned?

Much to some of my readers chagrins my next few books will not be Zombie Fallout 7. My next release will be Tim 2 which is a zombie apocalypse through the eyes of an aware zombie. He's an assh***. Then I'm working on a collaboration with John O'Brien and the book I am currently writing is an entirely new series entitled Lycan Fallout.

What was the best piece of advice you ever received about writing?

Armand Rosamilia, fellow writer, confidante and more importantly friend once wrote that there is no such thing as writer's block. He went on into much more eloquent prose but basically it boiled down to, 'It's just a matter of tuning out the rest of the world and spending time on your craft'. I can't tell you how many times I thought about that sage advice.

Finally before we let you go. Do you have a piece of advice for our readers who are looking to improve their writing?

Get an editor! Do not under any circumstances think you can do it on your own. Other than that, the old adage practice makes perfect is correct is this instance as well. The more you write the better you get. To think that the first time you tap out a story you're going to get the Iliad is unrealistic. And most importantly write because you have a story to tell, if you think you're going to write a book and be filthy rich like J.K. Rowlings you're in it for the wrong reasons. This is by no means a get rich quick scheme.

Thank you very much for spending time with us Mark, we hope the next book is a hit and we look forward to seeing Zombie Fallout on the big screen.

Thank you very much for the opportunity to ramble in your magazine, it has been an honor!

www.marktufo.com

"Where The Horror Happens" with Richard Thomas

We are pleased to be sitting down with writer Richard Thomas. He has written many short stories and three novels; Transubstantiate, Herniated Roots, and Staring Into the Abyss

So what is your workspace like?

I finally got my office all set up about a year ago. We had a large formal dining room that we never really used, so we turned it into a more informal dining room and then walled off a nice 12x12 office with French doors and bookcases lining the walls. I like to be surrounded by dark wood, and the books that inspire me. I got a new iMac last year, too, when my old eMac became obsolete. But when I'm really writing and doing my job well, the world falls away, the whole "body without organs" sensation that French philosopher Gilles Deleuze talked about.

Do you have a go-to gadget / app or service that you cannot live without?

I'd say my iMac, but really, Duotrope.com is a service that is invaluable to me. I write a lot of short stories, and it's such a great place to do research and keep track of where my submissions are. I currently have 97 submissions out, everything from fantasy and science fiction to horror and neo-noir to magical realism and literary fiction. There is no way I could keep track without them. I don't mind the new $50 a year fee they charge, I donated that much a year (or more) anyway. It keeps me busy while my agent is shopping my second book, Disintegration, it keeps me from pulling my hair out.

Do you have a set routine while you work?

Aside from blocking the world out, no, I don't have a set routine. No touchstones or mumbled prayers, no voodoo dolls are sacrifices in the back yard. I just try to stay focused on the subject matter at hand. I don't plot, but try to tap into an idea, a philosophy, an emotion. Sometimes I'll start with a word, or a picture, or a scene. Often I try to write about risky subjects, things that make me uncomfortable, whether it's sex or violence or just the truth. I like to write about the grotesque, those moments in our lives where we are at a tipping point, a situation that defines our character—and usually those moments are challenging, dark, and intense. I don't tend to write about going to work and shopping for groceries, coming home to kiss the kids.

__What is the best piece of advice you have ever received?__

The one piece of advice I've heard over and over again, from Stephen King to Richard Bausch, is read. If you're going to write, you need to read. It's important to study the masters in every genre you write, as well as stay current on what is happening in literature. You get to see how the truly gifted write, absorb their genius, and then try to apply that to you own work. You can study the storytelling of Stephen King, the lyric prose of Clive Barker, and the visceral and emotional violence of Jack Ketchum— and then let that inform your work. So, I'm always reading. That, and try to write emotional truths—speak from the heart, and be honest, because that will resonate with your readers. Everyone has a family, traditional or dysfunctional, and that helps to create our histories. Everyone has been in love, had lustful feelings, longed for something, been jealous—use those raw elements to help drive your work and keep the reader involved. But leave room for them to fill in the gaps, and be part of the narrative.

__Do you have a final piece of advice for our readers?__

Support new and struggling voices however you can, otherwise they will disappear. It can be something as small as retweeting a book release, or sharing a new book cover on your Facebook page. Put money in your budget for new authors, or pick up an anthology and if a particular author really blows you away, see if they have other work out there. Write kind and generous reviews of novels and collections that you love, at Amazon and Goodreads, because that way, those authors have a shot at succeeding. I know, I buy books by King and Straub and Ketchum and Barker, but I also love supporting lesser known authors like Brian Keene, Stephen Graham Jones, Paul Tremblay, and Kealan Patrick Burke—their work impacts me as much as the big guys, but I know that my support means more to them, it affects their sales and ability to keep writing when I promote work of theirs that I love. Don't be false, but don't be stingy with your words, right?

About *Richard Thomas:*

Richard is the author of three books—Transubstantiate, Herniated Roots, and Staring Into the Abyss. He was the winner of contests at ChiZine, One Buck Horror and Jotspeak, and has received five Pushcart Prize nominations to date. He has published 75 stories, including placement in Shivers VI (Cemetery Dance) with Stephen King and Peter Straub, PANK, Gargoyle, Weird Fiction  Review, Pear Noir!, and Opium. In his spare time he writes for The Nervous Breakdown and LitReactor. His is represented by Paula Munier at Talcott Notch. Visit him at whatdoesnotkillme.com for more information.

**If you have any feedback or would like to leave a
review please head over to Amazon and share your
thoughts about Sanitarium.**

**Thank you for your time and we salute your
love for all things horror.**

https://www.facebook.com/SanitariumPublishing

https://www.thesanitarium.co.uk/

https://twitter.com/sanitariumlit

https://www.instagram.com/sanitariumpublishing/